When a Woman's Fed Up

KEAIDY BENNETT

NENSHIA DANIELS

OTHER BOOKS BY KEAIDY BENNETT

Charge it to the Game

Charge it to the Game 2: Tammy's Story

Charge it to the Game 3: Three Sides to Every Story

Charge it to the Game 4: Pride Comes B4 Destruction (Coming 2024)

Somewhere Between Love & Misunderstanding

The Chronicles of a Love Addict

Shut Up & Finish Your Book Already

Don't Let the System Beat You

She Fell in Love with a Boss

The Business They Stood On (Coming 2024)

JOIN OUR MAILING LIST!

Don't miss out when we release new books! Make sure to join our mailing list by visiting lexxikhanpresents.com/join.

LexxiKhan Presents Publishing
www.LexxiKhanPresents.com

Ordering Information:
Quantity sales. Special discounts are available on quantity purchases by corporations, associations, and others. For details, contact the publisher at the web address above.

Content Advisory: "When a Woman's Fed Up" explores themes that include domestic violence, child abuse, and prostitution, which may be triggering to individuals on their healing journey. The authors and the publisher want to acknowledge the potential emotional impact these topics may have. If you find the content unsettling or if it resonates with personal experiences, we strongly encourage you to prioritize your well-being. Seek assistance from support networks, helplines, or professionals available to you. Remember, you are not alone, and help is accessible for those who need it.

This book contains an excerpt from "Charge it to the Game 4: Pride Comes B4 Destruction." It may be edited or deleted prior to actual publication.

ISBN-13: 978-1-958335-18-5

DEDICATION

For the woman who allowed someone to play in her face too long.

Fatal Investment

NENSHIA DANIALS

BANG! They both took a deep breath. *BANG!* Brenda's ears rang as she stumbled three feet to the bathtub and rested her tired body on the edge. Her eyes filled with tears, blood gloving both her hands. She dropped the gun...

1

ADDICTED TO FANTASIES

The first time he saw Brenda McClain was on a Monday. Mondays were her favorite days. He watched through the window as she made her way across the parking lot, hopping over puddles created in the spring rain. He was intrigued by her youthful nature.

Barging into the café doors, Brenda shook her umbrella dry and rushed through the café to the back. "Good morning," she smiled as she walked by his table. He gave a polite nod of acknowledgment and allowed the moment to breathe before he turned, watching her until the 'Employee's Only' door obstructed his view as it closed behind her.

"It's Money Monday!" Brenda said excitedly. Sam had just arrived moments before, and they both rushed to put on their hair nets and wash their hands.

"If you say so. I'm not as addicted to fantasies as you are, so it's just Monday for me," Sam smugly replied.

"I'll take fantasy over misery any day. You're just as bitter as an unclaimed baby-momma," Brenda laughed as she looked in the mirror, ensuring her collar was straight.

"Who's the guy sitting at table 12? His face looks familiar, but I can't place it," Brenda asked.

"That's not my table. Why would I know who's sitting at it?" Sam answered.

"Because you're nosey and watch all the tables," Brenda clarified.

They emerged on the floor and scanned the dining room. The busy Monday traffic at the café was heavier than usual. They both smiled with anticipation of hefty tips in the morning rush. Being nosey, Sam looked over to table 12.

"Oh, that guy always sits in the back corner in Tasha's section. I don't know why he's sitting by the window today. I hear he's a good tipper, though," Sam shrugged, informing Brenda before they parted ways to work their tables.

"Good Morning, sir. It's a good day to have breakfast at NuBees cafe! What can I get for you?" Brenda smiled. She was being as fake as the day is long, but even her disingenuous smile was beautiful enough to capture his attention.

"Are you this friendly to all your customers?" he asked, looking down at his menu.

"Only to the ones who are as handsome as you," Brenda flirted.

"Or only to the ones that Tasha tells you tip well?" he said as he lifted his head to make eye contact with her. Brenda was busted, and the only response she could think of was to snap out how Tasha hadn't told her anything. Technically, Sam did, so she gave a halfhearted laugh and lifted her notepad and pen to indicate her readiness to take his order.

Assured in the accuracy of his assessment by her lack of response, he continued, "So waitresses and strippers scout the floors the same, huh?"

Not sure if his statement was meant to be an insult, Brenda cautiously asserted, "We have assigned tables, so there is not much to scout. But like strippers, if you prefer certain waitresses, I can get permission for Tasha to serve you."

"No need. I'm sitting in your section today. You will serve me today. Two eggs, an English muffin, and a small coffee," he asserted.

Brenda confirmed his order. "Coming right up," she said as she walked away. A few seconds passed, and he turned again to admire the entirety of her short, curvy frame, his imagination defining lines that could not be seen through her black slacks and loose-fitted work shirt. Tasha and Brenda crossed paths for the first time.

"Hey, Tasha! It's Money Monday!" Brenda greeted her.

"I know, right? And I see one of my regulars is sitting in your section today. He's weird, but just be polite, and he usually tips $20 plus the change from his food," Tasha coached.

"Yeah, he said earlier waitresses and strippers work the floor the same, and I was only being nice because you told me he tips well," Brenda stated.

Tasha laughed. "Go get your tips," she said, giving Brenda a playful tap on the titty. They both walked away with a staged haste as they noticed their manager's car drive into the parking lot.

"Would you like cream and sugar for your coffee, sir?" Brenda asked as she placed his breakfast in front of him and poured his coffee.

"Yes, please. Two of each. And I am left-handed, so place my coffee and utensils appropriately going forward," he stated.

"Yes, sir," Brenda promptly replied, correcting the curious look on her face before her manager walked by. Amid the hustle and bustle of the Monday morning rush, Sam and Brenda got a momentary break at the counter as they waited for their next orders to come up.

"Table 12 is weird. His beard is shaved too perfectly, and he told me to set his table left-handed going forward," Brenda gossiped to Sam.

"Going forward? So he has a new seat now?" Sam joked. "At least you don't have to deal with that one kid who thinks farting is funny. I'm just waiting on the day he sharts instead of farts." They laughed and took their orders to their tables.

"How was your breakfast?" Brenda asked as she handed him the black leather receipt holder.

"It was fine. Thank you. Bring me a cup of ice water to go, please," he requested.

"Yes, sir," Brenda complied. Returning promptly, walking up from behind as he put on his jacket, Brenda said, "Excuse me. Here's your water, sir."

"Thank you. You can keep the change as part of your tip. Have a good day," he said as he took the water from Brenda's outstretched hand and left the café. Brenda took the receipt holder and placed it in her pocket as she cleaned the table before cashing out all her customers. She opened the leather holder from Table 12. The meal was $5.17. He had paid for the meal with a hundred-dollar bill and left a twenty-dollar tip.

"Sam! Psssssst, Sam!" Brenda whispered loudly across the serving counter.

"What?" Sam yelled back.

"Come here. And shh!" Brenda said.

"How you expect to have a private conversation in the middle of a café floor, I don't understand. But we can whisper if that makes you feel better," Sam said.

"Just shut up and listen. Do you think Tasha would do something strange for a little piece of change?" Brenda asked softly, lowering her chin and speaking into Sam's chest.

Sam burst into laughter at the question, "I don't know Tasha to know what's strange or what can be done for solid bills over change. Where is this craziness coming from?" Sam asked.

"Weirdo at table 12 left me a twenty-dollar tip, AND he let me keep the change from his meal!" Brenda explained.

"So, what's the…" Sam started.

"His meal was $5.17, and he paid with a hundred-dollar bill," Brenda, wide-eyed, interrupted.

"Oh, yeah. You just sold some vagina. What did you do when he handed it to you?" Sam asked.

"He didn't hand it to me. He asked me to go get him some water. I did. When I came back, I handed him the water, and he told me to keep the change and have a good day. He just left the receipt book on the table," Brenda defended herself.

"Oh, he's smooth. He bought you and left before you even knew you had been bought," Sam laughed.

"He hasn't bought anything!" Brenda said as she processed his receipt with the twenty-dollar bill, keeping only the change from that as a tip. She folded and placed the hundred-dollar bill in her back pocket and rushed back out to the floor to return receipts and credit cards and prepare for her next round of tables.

Her shift ended, and Brenda smiled as she tiredly plopped down into the front seat of her car. She counted two hundred and six dollars in the rainy parking lot. It had been a great Monday for her. Suddenly she remembered him and the hundred-dollar bill resting in her back pocket. His tip was almost half of what she had earned the entire day. She took the folded bill and placed it in her glove compartment. Too prideful to keep it, she kept it in her car to return it whenever she saw him again.

2
DIRTY MONEY

Twenty-three years old and full of youth, beauty, optimism, and ambition, Brenda worked hard at Café NuBees. There were stories of business owners and executives hiring out of NuBees for positions that could open countless doors. There were also stories of NuBees being a hiring pool for glorified assistants. Either way, Brenda was positive that she was in the right place to land a job. She dreamed of being an architect and was almost done with her schooling; she worked at the café hoping to meet someone who could employ her by the time she graduated.

It was another Monday, and shortly after she arrived for her shift, Table 12 walked in the door. She noticed his frame and positively recognized him as he sat down at table 12. Before clocking in, she ran out to her car and grabbed the folded bill that had been sitting in her glove compartment for a week. Finally, she could get rid of this dirty money.

"It must have been good! He's sitting back at table 12!" Sam taunted Brenda as she rushed around the counter to get an order.

"Shut up!" Brenda laughed back in agitation.

"Good morning, sir. Before I take your order, I have something that belongs to you," Brenda announced as she placed the folded hundred-dollar bill on the table near his left hand. "I want to make sure it's as easy as possible for you to pick back up what you dropped last week."

He smirked, "I didn't drop this. I remember placing this in a receipt book to pay for my meal."

"Yes, sir. But your meal was only $5.17. There is a thin line between generosity and propositioning. And I do not have any vagina for sale, so like I said, I'm returning what you dropped last week. Now what can I get for you?" Brenda asked.

"Okay. I'll have wheat toast, a bowl of fruit, two eggs, and a small coffee," the man replied with a bit of laughter. The notion that she plainly accused him of soliciting tickled him.

"Yes, sir," Brenda said as she walked away quickly, not to engage in any further conversation.

Returning with his breakfast, Brenda placed his coffee and utensils to his left and, for confirmation, asked, "Two creams and two sugars, right?"

"That's correct. Thank you," Table 12 answered.

This Monday was slower than most, and noticing Brenda cleaning tables with no other customers to serve, Table 12 motioned her over to his table.

"Yes, sir? How can I help you?" Brenda asked politely.

"I would like a cup of ice water to go, please," he requested.

"Sure. I'll be right back," Brenda responded.

Noticing she had not left the receipt holder, he stopped her. "Excuse me. Do you have my ticket prepared already?" He asked.

"No, sir. I'll bring it back with your water," Brenda stated.

He smirked as he recognized Brenda's attempt to assert some authority. At her return, he stood and grabbed the receipt holder and water from Brenda.

"Thank you for your service," he stated as he watched Brenda watch him place a twenty-dollar bill into the holder to pay for his meal. "Keep the change as part of your tip," he said as he walked off with a smug grin. Feeling as though she had established control in her exchange at table 12, Brenda cashed out the ticket and kept the change from the twenty as a tip. Returning to clean off the table, Brenda rolled her eyes and quickly scanned the parking lot to see if Table 12 was, by chance, still outside. She didn't know what type of car he drove and did not see his familiar frame anywhere in the parking lot. He must have been gone. Under his plate were ten new hundred-dollar bills, the folded one she had returned to him earlier, and a card with a phone number and 'proposition' written on it. Outraged, Brenda asked for a break and stormed to her car to call the number.

"Hello," Table 12 answered after the third ring.

"I don't know who you think you are, but you really must be stupid to try and buy sex and leave evidence. I can call the police right now and report you!" Brenda argued.

"Well, that would be stupid if I propositioned you for sex. Would you like to calm down and hear the proposition, or are you committed to the rage of your assumption?" Table 12 calmly replied. Her silence and heavy, angered breathing gave him permission to continue.

"I'd like to give you a job. I would require that you start immediately. The thousand dollars is a sign-on bonus if you take the position. It is an executive assistant position and would require some travel," he offered.

"Executive of what?" Brenda inquired.

"A business," he said sharply.

"When you say immediately, what exactly do you mean? No, wait. This is weird! I don't even know your name. Come get your money and stop being weird before I call the police on you!" she said.

"Okay. No problem. I'll see you shortly," he stated and hung up the phone. About one minute later, as Brenda still sat in her car trying to process the conversation, Table 12 emerged from the back of a black Suburban. He was being chauffeured, and as the driver closed the door behind him, Brenda jumped out of her car to catch his attention before he entered the café.

"Hey! Proposition guy! Over here!" she yelled.

He turned and smiled with delight that Brenda was outside the café where the pressures of the environment were relieved. He walked over and greeted her with a simple head nod as she unfolded her arms to hand him the eleven hundred dollars he had left on the table.

"Here's your money, and you should stop sitting in my section when you come here," Brenda demanded.

"You have a bold mouth, don't you?" he laughed.

"And you have a bold attitude to think I'm going to be propositioned for anything by a complete stranger," she snapped back.

"I simply observed some traits in you that would serve my business well and offered an opportunity," he responded.

"You didn't even tell me your name or what you do," Brenda said.

"I am a veterinarian, and you can call me Sir. Yes, Sir; no, Sir; Mr. Sir, whatever feels right for you," Sir said.

Brenda squinted her eyes and thought through the situation. What type of veterinarian has a chauffeur? She was convinced, "You fit the exact profile of an introverted functioning sociopathic murderer. No vet can afford a chauffeur, and nobody's momma would really name them Sir. Excuse me, Sir. I need to get back to work." Brenda closed and locked her car door and pushed past Sir to head back into the cafe.

Sir gently grabbed her hand as she walked past, "You are assertive and bold. I like that. It can serve you well in business, but only if you are in an environment that will teach how."

Brenda looked down at her hand in disapproval at the physical contact and politely pulled away.

"I have to get to work. Have a nice day," she said softly as she turned to walk towards the café.

"You do the same," Sir smiled as he waved for his door to be opened.

Brenda was altogether excited, offended, suspicious, hopeful, and angry. Was this real life? What she wanted was left under a plate of toast crumbs with bait money. She had imagined a job opportunity coming through months of conversations leading to an invitation to apply. Under a plate, though? She rushed back into the café and washed up to prepare to serve the next table. Lost in thought, trying to unconfuse her feelings on the morning interaction she had had with Sir, Brenda half-heartedly finished her shift and drove home.

When she pulled into the parking space of her apartment, she let her seat back and stared at the dotted details of the cloth ceiling of the car.

"I don't want to get trafficked, Lord. If this man is a pimp, please weaken his hand. It feels so strong right now," Brenda prayed as she gently rubbed the palm of her hand where Sir had held her. His touch was memorable because it was strong but gentle. When he grabbed her hand, he did it so softly but restrained her with such ease. He handled her as a doll that he might break if he touched her with his power. After a full shift of thoughts and trusting in her pimp protection prayer, Brenda picked up her phone. It was 4:28 p.m., still business hours. She redialed the number. It rang two times.

"Hello, Brenda," Sir said directly.

"Hello, Sir," Brenda replied.

"Are you calling to accept my proposition?" Sir quickly questioned before Brenda could say a word.

"Yes. As long as I can get clarification on some things. What is the formal interview process? What are my job responsibilities? What is my pay rate? And can I get direct deposit?" Brenda snapped back.

"I will text you an address you will report to at 9 a.m. Be dressed professionally, and be sure to have your I.D. and an updated resume. Your job responsibilities will include anything needed to assist me in my role as an executive. Your pay rate will be negotiated at the time of your formal interview based on your interview and resume. Establishing direct deposit is standard practice immediately upon hire. Is there anything else you need clarification on?" Sir asked.

"No, Sir. Thank you. Have a good evening," Brenda said with a puff of authority.

"You have a nice evening as well," Sir subtly laughed back.
Sir enjoyed frustrating Brenda, and she knew it. She closed her eyes and took a deep breath before allowing herself to release a huge smile. She had an actual job interview in the morning! Brenda made up her mind that she would take a cautious chance at this opportunity.

3
PIMP PRAYERS

It was 8:45 a.m. as Brenda was sitting in the lobby of the beautiful downtown high-rise, her GPS guided her to from Sir's text message. Googling the address the night before only to find that the building is a multi-use business space for hundreds of businesses, Brenda watched the early traffic come in and out of the building as she waited for her 9 a.m. appointment. Not even a service dog in sight. This was the least animal-friendly veterinary setup she had ever seen.

"Hello, ma'am. Are you here for a 9 a.m.?" the office attendant asked.

"Yes, ma'am. Brenda?" Brenda clarified.

"Yes. Right this way," the office attendant confirmed.

Brenda picked up her resume holder and hand-ironed her blazer and slacks as she followed the office attendant down the marble halls to the elevators. They entered the empty elevator, and the attendant pressed the button for the 40th floor. *Bing.* They exited the elevator, and the office attendant guided Brenda down a hall to another set of elevators.

"Take this elevator to the 50th floor and wait in the lobby. You will be called in for your interview from there. You are free to access the breakfast Danishes and coffee," the attendant politely nodded as she turned to go back to the elevators.

"Thank you," Brenda said as she nervously entered the elevator.

She pushed the button for the 50th floor and took long, deep breaths to calm her shaking body. The possibility of a big opportunity and the fear of the unknown overtook her nerves.

Bing.

The elevator doors opened, and Brenda confidently walked into the beautiful and completely empty lobby of the 50th floor. An oversized receptionist desk was the first noticeable thing. The entire space was filled with natural light as no walls obstructed the extensive glass sidings on either end of the room. There was a welcoming breakfast display of Danishes, fruits, muffins, orange juice, and coffee. This was not a veterinarian's office. The oversized chairs to the left of the breakfast display were set in front of a glass table with several business magazines. Opting out of breakfast for fear of anything being set on her nervous stomach, Brenda sat in front of the glass table and began browsing the reading selections. Maybe she could gain some insight into what type of business this was. She was not given much time to investigate.

"Good morning," a familiar voice echoed through the lobby.

Brenda stood up, "Sir."

Sir walked towards her, extending his hand in greeting, "Thank you for being prompt for your interview. Come this way, please."

Brenda followed Sir through a door adjacent to the oversized and unattended receptionist's desk. It was a long hallway with small private office spaces about every fifteen feet. They arrived at the seventh office space.

"Do you have your resume and I.D.?" Sir asked.

"Yes, Sir," Brenda replied as she handed him her resume folder with her I.D. placed in the holder's business card slot.

"Good. This is your interview room. Your interview will start when you click the start button on the computer. You have two hours," Sir instructed as he nodded and continued down the hall.

Brenda entered the interview room, delighted at the ambiance. The lighting was easy on the eyes, the soft green color selection of the décor was calming, and the clean, fresh-smelling air was pleasant. Brenda sat in the desk chair and clicked start. The interview process seemed as straightforward and normal as any executive assistant job interview. It started with a typing test, then a virtual interactive scheduling test, and several 'what would you do' questions to establish a baseline assessment of personality. An hour and a half later, Brenda was finished. Looking at the time and seeing how early she had completed the interview, Brenda stepped into the hallway to see if there was anyone she could notify of her early finish. There was no one. She sat back down at the desk in the interview room and elected to just wait. A few moments later, there was a gentle knock on the door. Before slowly pushing it open, Sir was back.

"I see you finished a bit early. Good. Your resume and background screening have been processed. Come with me to my office, and we will discuss the results of your interview," Sir stated as he held the door open for Brenda to pass.

"You told me you were a veterinarian, and I haven't seen one animal since I've come into this building. What type of anti-animal veterinarian are you?" Brenda gently jabbed, unable to hold her curiosity in as they walked down a long, uniform hallway.

"I am a veterinarian. I have other businesses also. This is one of the others," Sir replied curtly, letting Brenda know this was not a topic where more conversation was invited.

Brenda let the need for her satisfaction go at that time. The entire process of this interview was beyond anything she had experienced before. The cost of the breakfast display in the lobby would satisfy a whole day's pay for her. She would let this go for the sake of a job.

They finally reached the end of the hallway and a set of beautifully detailed French doors. He placed his palm on the scanner outside the doors, and the left side door slowly opened. He motioned her to enter the office before him and instructed her to sit in the seat in front of his presidential-style office desk. Brenda sat down with a straightened back and crossed her ankles. Sir walked around to the chair of his desk and sat down as he slid Brenda's resume holder closer to him. A small jump from Brenda as the click of the automatic door behind her closed gave Sir a smile.

"I can leave the door open if it makes you more comfortable," Sir offered.

"That would be great. It would make me much more relaxed," Brenda accepted.

Without hesitation, Sir placed his hand on a scanner on the left side of this desk, and one of the two French doors opened back up. He smiled and returned his attention to the resume folder on his desk.

"Tell me about your professional ambitions, Miss McClain. I see you are in school for architecture. What is it that you want to build?" Sir asked.

"My goal right now is to position myself to learn the business. Ultimately, I would like to bring a more creative and functional aspect of design to architecture. Build buildings that are more cost-effective and functional through designs like water collection roofs as standard to promote self-sufficiency," Brenda confidently responded.

"Ok. This position requires a lot of traveling, non-traditional work hours, and for you to start today. Is that going to be a problem?"

"No, Sir," Brenda replied.

"Good. I would like to extend an offer as a salaried employee for fifty-two thousand a year with four weeks of paid vacation and three sick days. Your living, travel, and healthcare costs are corporate expenses, and a company card will be issued to cover expenses incurred during working hours," Sir detailed.

"Sounds fair," Brenda stated as she tried to mask her excitement.

"Good. Sir instructed. You may return to the lobby, and an attendant will assist you in registering your company card and provide you with your schedule beginning today."

"Thank you," Brenda said as she stood up and politely dismissed herself.

No sooner than the door closed behind her, Brenda raised her hands up to the sky and gave a silent yell. This will be the most money she's ever made, the best benefits she's ever had, and it starts today! Making her way down the hall, she composed herself and took a deep breath before walking through the door back into the lobby. The oversized receptionist desk was now being attended by a tall, dark, and broad-shouldered man. He was not the stereotypical desk attendant. He was attractive, looked strong, and had a presence about himself.

"Good morning. I am Adam. I will assist you in getting your company card activated and making you aware of your schedule," the attendant said.

"Good morning. I am..." Brenda started.

"Brenda. I know," Adam interrupted. "Please enter a four-digit pin code," he requested as he placed a keypad on the desk in front of Brenda.

She entered her pin code and listened for further instruction as Adam neatly placed two folders on the desk beside the keypad.

"This is your employment contract and employee benefits package. And this is a tentative schedule for the next five days. Details of your daily assignments will be communicated as tasks are assigned. Please review it carefully and let me know if you have any questions," Adam said as he slid the folders closer to Brenda, encouraging her to review the information right away.

Brenda gave a polite thank you before retiring to the lobby's seating section. She opened the employment folder first. As expected, all the details discussed were in the documents. Standard non-compete and non-disclosure forms were included. Satisfied with the information presented, Brenda extracted the documents requiring a signature from the package and signed them. Closing the folder and placing the signature pages on top, Brenda slid the folder to the side and picked up the schedule folder. Her eyes widened as she looked at her next five days.

Tuesday – Arrive in Lisbon, Portugal 7 a.m. Day assignment TBD.

Wednesday – Day assignment TBD. Depart Lisbon, Portugal, 4:30 p.m. Arrive in Madrid, Spain, 5:50 p.m.

Thursday – Day assignment TBD.

Friday – Depart Madrid, Spain, 6 a.m. Arrive in Paris, France, 8:05 a.m. Day assignment TBD.

Saturday – Day assignment TBD. Departing Paris, France, 8:55 p.m.

Not one of her destinations would be a returning trip. Brenda was stuck in a state of excitement and shock. After her heart stopped racing and the adrenaline pumping from the information she just processed, common sense and fear brought some balance to the excitement.

"First week and my employer is willing to blow this much of a bag? Travel benefits before I ever copied a piece of paper, scheduled an appointment, or even answered a phone call? Nope! Something ain't right. This is definitely a pre-trafficking interview," Brenda whispered to herself as she looked over and noticed Adam's intense gaze on her. He immediately broke his stare and redirected his attention to the tablet on his desk. Not to make the moment awkward, Brenda acknowledged his attention.

"I am almost done reviewing the schedule, then I have a couple of questions," she said.

"Yes, ma'am. Whenever you're ready," Adam responded.

A few moments later, Brenda gathered the folders and returned to the receptionist's desk, where Adam was seated. He respectfully stood as she approached.

"Before I give you these forms, I have a couple of questions," Brenda asserted.

Adam gave her a head nod to continue.

"I see that there is a conduct exception for social media and a privacy policy that may limit what company-related information we are permitted to post. Are my location and activities abroad, outside of working hours, considered company-related information that would be restricted?" Brenda asked.

"No. Outside of working hours when abroad is your time. You are permitted to post whatever personal, non-company related content you wish," Adam answered.

"Okay, great, because I'm posting where I'm at, what I'm doing, and when I should be doing it again on all my social media platforms in case this is a whole trafficking job offer situation," Brenda bluntly told Adam as his eyes stretched, and a tiny bit of laughter escaped in shock at the notion.

Brenda continued, "And I see on the schedule that I will be picked up from my home address this afternoon to prepare to leave for my first assignment. And who exactly is picking me up from my home?"

"Me," Adam stated shortly, glancing down at his watch, fully displaying his urgency for Brenda to get home and prepare for the schedule that would be starting in just a matter of hours.

"Oh. Well, thank you for your clarification. I'll be on my way so that I will be ready when you arrive to fulfill my duties for the rest of the day," Brenda said as she handed Adam the signature pages of her employee package.

"Thank you," Adam responded.

"Thank you, too. I'll see you shortly," Brenda said, hurrying to leave for her interview and prepare for her new job.

4
LET'S GO

It was 11:30 a.m., and Brenda had been instructed to be prepared for travel by 6 p.m. Brenda had never been to Europe, had no idea what to pack, and her hair was not at all in a European tour-appropriate state. Six and a half hours to pack, pamper, and do hair. Brenda is black. This was impossible. On the commute home, Brenda talked through her game plan of how she could multitask to be as ready as possible by 6 p.m.

Stumbling over the door frame as she rushed into her apartment, Brenda went straight to the bathroom to set her emergency get fine supplies on the counter. Deep conditioner, three brushes, two combs, a bag of hair clips, a razor, tweezers, seven different oils, deodorant, mascara, lip gloss, and a blunt. Mary Jane always helped ease her anxiety and focus her mind. Superpowers activated. Brenda turned the shower on and let the water run to get hot as she went into her closet to get her cosmetic travel bag. As she used her get fine supplies, she would throw them in the bag. Multitasking at its finest. Reentering a steam-filled bathroom, she grabbed the detangling brush and conditioner to begin the most difficult task ahead of her. High-minded, the pulses of hot water beating against her skin felt like a warm waterfall and instantly relaxed Brenda's body. Tilting her head back, she closed her eyes and let the hard pressing droplets massage her scalp as they saturated her curls. The combination of steam and massaging water pressure took Brenda's body where her mind tried not to go.

Eyes closed, nipples erect, Brenda began to picture Sir's tall and dominating frame. He was attractive, well-groomed, and assertive.

What young woman, baited with life dreams and opportunity, wouldn't fantasize about his intentions?

She turned around. Clearing the water from her face, eyes still closed, Brenda tilted her head back again. The pressure of the hot droplets beating against her erect nipples activated every womanly sense in her body. Her flower tightened, and juices began to flow, thinking about what Sir may have wanted and how he wanted it. She cupped her breasts with one hand and massaged herself with the other. It had been a long while since Brenda had felt the satisfaction of a man, and just the thought of penetration excited her almost to climax. She rubbed and imagined and rubbed some more. The temperature of her juices, compared to the hot water beating against her body, created a cool spot. She pulled the shower head down to feel the pressure more directly. A few short moments later, she braced herself against the shower wall, her passions pouring out as she felt her heart beating at the meeting of her thighs.

Her physical, now satisfied through imagination, Brenda finished washing her head hair and shaving the rest. With no time to spare, she hopped out of the shower, cleared the steam from her mirror with a quick swipe, set her curls, then oiled her body down. Looking over at the clock, she had managed to finish her hair and full body skincare routine in just an hour and a half. Her superpowers were in high gear. For the sake of time, Brenda opted to pack dresses and jumpers. One-and-done outfits were the only way she was going to be packed in time to still squeeze in a nail refresh and eyebrow waxing before Adam was set to arrive. Completely packed in only two bags, she quickly slipped into a sundress and slides and dropped her bags near the door as she rushed to her favorite nail salon. Calling ahead during the commute, God was shining on her. Peter was working and available for an appointment in thirty minutes. She made a quick stop at the smoothie shop and made it right on time for her full set, pedicure, and eyebrow waxing.

Adam was set to arrive in about forty minutes. The salon was only twenty minutes away, and she was walking out of the door. Mission accomplished. Brenda drove home, less rushed, thinking about what she would wear for today's travel. Though sundresses were comfortable, wearing one on the first day of the job was not the best idea. As she pulled up to her apartment, she noticed a black Tahoe parked out front. It was Adam. He was already there, standing beside the truck scrolling through his phone. Looking at her clock, she still had fourteen minutes to spare before he was supposed to arrive.

"Hey, Adam! You're a little early," Brenda said as she greeted him, stepping out of her car.

"And you look like you're going to be a little late," Adam said, observing the casual dress she was wearing.

"I'll be on time. I'm already packed. Give me a few minutes to change, and I'll be ready to go," Brenda replied.

"Yes, ma'am," Adam said as he watched her walk into her apartment, ass jiggling in all its glory.

A few minutes later, Brenda emerged from her apartment in a comfortable, neat tracksuit and tennis shoes. She placed her bags outside the door and turned to go back inside to turn the air off before leaving. Adam gathered her bags, put them in the rear of the truck, and opened the door for Brenda to be seated in the back seat.

"Thank you," she said as her short frame climbed into the truck.

Adam gave her a polite "You're welcome" as he closed the door and got in the driver's seat to be on their way.

Twenty minutes later, they arrived at the office. Turning in, Brenda recognized Sir's frame standing at the roundabout with one bag in his hand. Adam pulled up, parked the car, and got out to load Sir's bags into the trunk. Adam opened the rear door, and Sir stood outside the truck for a few moments, examining Brenda from head to toe. His still face gave no indication of disapproval of her appearance.

"Hello again, Brenda. Glad to see that you are punctual, especially on your first day," Sir said as he sat down, and Adam closed the door.

"Yes, Sir. This is a job, right? I would be nothing less than punctual, especially on my first day," Brenda sarcastically responded.

"Adam. How many bags total do we have?" Sir asked.

"Three, Sir," Adam answered.

"Traveling through Europe, and you only have two bags? Good," Sir rhetorically addressed Brenda. "Read over these documents during our travel time so when we land you will be prepared to complete your assignments," Sir continued as he handed Brenda a folder.

"Yes, Sir," Brenda said as she received the folder.

The ride to the airport was void of conversation. The world news radio station filled what would have been a still and awkward silence. Adam turned off onto a side street before reaching the main airport entrance. Brenda, noticing the detour, became flushed with anxiety.

This was it. She was being trafficked. After about two miles of riding, they turned into a small parking lot with a metal frame building. Finding a parking space, Adam turned off the engine, popped the trunk, and got out to open the door for Sir and Brenda to exit. Sir grabbed his bag from the trunk. Seeing there were three bags left, Brenda reached to grab one of her bags.

"I have it. Please, stand over there," Adam stopped her.

"I can get one of my bags," Brenda laughed off Adam's request as she leaned forward to grab one of her bags.

"Brenda. He has it. Let's go," Sir sternly said to Brenda.

"Okay. Yes, Sir," Brenda complied as she gave Adam a jovial wide-eyed look at the sternness of Sir, who was now walking towards the entrance of the building.

If she was being trafficked, this was his chance to wink and help save her life in exchange for less prison time. Brenda had been to the airport several times and had never known there to be this side street or this building. Adam ignored her eye contact, grabbed the rest of the bags, closed the trunk, and began towards the building at the sound of the horn confirming the truck was locked. During the short hundred-foot walk to the door, Brenda nervously looked around and cataloged details as she checked her pocket to ensure she had her phone. The glass sliding doors opened, and Brenda's suspicions eased as a man in a tailored bellhop suit stood on the other side of the door.

"Welcome. Please allow me," the attendant greeted them as he reached to relieve Sir and Adam of the bags.

"Thank you," Sir responded.

"Will you require a meal, shower, or dry-cleaning services before your flight?" the attendant asked.

"No, thank you. You can inform the pilot we are ready to depart as soon as possible," Sir instructed.

"Yes, Sir," confirmed the attendant with a polite head nod as he turned to wheel away the bags on the small carrier next to him.

Brenda followed Sir and Adam as they continued down a wide entryway with what seemed like low ceilings in respect to the outside appearance of the building. Maybe the bellhop was a hired actor, and this building has multiple floors of trafficker holding rooms, Brenda thought to herself as she cautiously continued. A few feet before the hallway was too long for Brenda to decide to turn around and make a run, the hallway ended and dramatically opened into a stunning lobby with thirty-foot ceilings. The center point of the entry was a single glass pane that framed a doorway opening to the visible private runway on the other side of the glass.

There was a sleek blue jet and two attendants checking the wheels of the machine as a fuel line ran from a side section of the building to the small plane. They were flying private. Sir took a seat in the oversized rounded chairs that lined the right wall of the open lobby as Adam proceeded toward the glass window of the runway. Reading the situation, Brenda followed Sir and sat professionally spaced beside him. She looked over and could see the attendant who had greeted them at the door rolling the cart containing their bags out to load the jet. Brenda patiently sat in anxious excitement. This day would be full of so many firsts. She was taking her first tour of Europe and her first private flight. Noticing Sir's focus on his reading material, Brenda opted not to disturb him with surface-level conversation and just soaked in the moment in silence.

A few short minutes later, Brenda noticed the fuel line being disconnected from the jet and rolled back in. It was nearing time to go. Adam walked over with a still and emotionless face.

"Excuse me. We can now begin boarding," Adam informed Sir.

"Thank you," Sir replied as he closed the folder he had been reviewing and straightened his clothes before standing to walk to the runway. A pilot emerged from the opposite side of the lobby just as Sir, Adam, and Brenda neared the glass doors opening to the runway. An attendant appeared and opened the doors. With the pilot leading the way, they all walked out to the jet.

"Good to see you! We have excellent conditions for flying, and I anticipate being on or ahead of schedule for today's travels."

"Good to hear," Sir responded. Noticing the pilot's glance at Brenda, Sir continued, "This is my assistant, Brenda. She will be traveling with us on assignment for a while."

"Nice to meet you, Brenda," the pilot said as he extended his hand to help Brenda step up into the small doorway of the jet.

"Likewise," Brenda replied, quickly breaking eye contact with the pilot's intense gaze. She was beautiful and knew how not to open the door to a man's visual interest. She was working. No time to flirt.

Settling in their seats, they all fastened their safety belts and listened as the pilot began to speak. "Wind conditions, favorable. Humidity and possibility of thunderstorms - low. Fuel level, full. Mechanical systems check, all clear. Communications systems, Alpha 2257 checking in. Can you hear me?" the pilot recited.

"Base 5312. Alpha 2257, we got you loud and clear. You are all clear for takeoff," a man responded on the speakers.

Because of how quickly the time seemed to be passing, they would be watching the sunset as they made their departure. The engines started, and the jet began its slow building of momentum down the runway. Brenda's chest tightened as she felt the speed of the jet increase. This was much different than a commercial flight. The propulsion and turbulence in this smaller vessel felt like she was on a ride at a theme park rather than a flight. She closed her eyes and rested her head back in an effort not to respond dramatically to this new situation. Throwing up and crying on the first day of work would not be a good look. Brenda opened her eyes on queue in response to the pilot's voice to see both Sir and Adam looking in amusement at her, releasing the pressure from her tightly closed eyes.

"We are in the air and on our way. In approximately thirteen hours, you will be looking at the beautiful sunrise of Lisbon, Portugal. Feel free to take in this lovely sunset and relax. Thank you for trusting me with your travels on this lovely evening, and enjoy your flight," the pilot announced.

With a deep exhale, Brenda unclamped her restraints and leaned forward to get her assignment folder from the small shoulder bag she carried. This was not a very talkative group, and she was technically working, so reviewing her assignments during the flight was only logical. The Sé de Lisboa, Terreiro do Paço, Castelo de São Jorge, Oriente Station, and Pavilhão de Portugal were on the itinerary for Lisbon. Brenda's assignment was to observe and take notes at each of these sites to determine the strongest design features of each of these unique buildings. These notes would then be compiled into a report of conceptual building ideas that could successfully translate to a functional design in an urban setting. This sounded fun. A few hours into reading the history of these buildings she was set to visit, Brenda's eyes got heavy, and she opted to get some rest for the remainder of the flight. She wasn't getting trafficked, and she was getting paid to take a tour of European architecture on a private jet. She apologized to God for every petty deed she had ever done and thanked Him for this opportunity before dozing off as she looked out over the thick night clouds.

5
I'M BEING AN EXPENSIVE HOE

"We will begin decent in approximately 10 minutes. Please secure your safety restraints and cover any loose foods or liquids," the pilot's voice announced through the speakers.

Brenda jerked awake, startled by the sound of the pilot's voice. They had arrived. She looked out the window and squinted at the beauty of the sun rising against the ocean line in the distance. The brightness was too much for her sleepy eyes, but she could not turn away and miss taking in the breathtaking scene. She continued to squint, eyes locked, as she blindly shuffled through her carrying bag, feeling for her shades. She found them and gave some reprieve to her eyes as she continued to take in the beauty of the descent into the city. The cobblestone streets were not yet bustling with life. As the jet got lower and lower, Brenda marveled at the architecture. So many old stone structures built seemingly right on top of one another, creating a maze of stone streets between them. It was beautiful, and she could not wait to explore it all.

"Transportation is confirmed as waiting now. Breakfast will be at Delta Q – Avenida da Liberdade, and check-in has been confirmed for all rooms at the Valverde Hotel," Adam updated Sir as the plane began to rumble as it took the slow dive down towards the runway.

"Great. Thank you," Sir acknowledged as he closed his carrying case and prepared for landing.

"Another great flight. You are all clear to release your safety restraints and exit the vessel. Thank you again for trusting me with your travel needs, and I'll see you all for departure tomorrow afternoon," the pilot said.

This was it. Brenda was about to take her first steps on European ground, and she was overwhelmed with excitement.

"Pardon me. If I could be excused to the powder room for just a moment before we get off, I'd appreciate it," Brenda sarcastically said in the most stereotypically high-class voice she could generate with her morning rasp.

"Powder room?" Sir rebutted with a smirk.

"Yes. I'm in Europe now. I don't piss, I tinkle, and it's a powder room, not a bath or restroom," Brenda said as she dabbed the slob from the side of her cheek and flipped her hair.

"You may be excused," Sir indulged her playful attitude.

Brenda took her morning tinkle and washed her hands and face before pulling out her travel-sized toothbrush and paste to top off her quick jet bathroom grooming routine. No way she was going to step off the plane with foul breath or crusty eyes. No telling what Portuguese dream boat was waiting to adore her. She emerged from the restroom a few moments later to see only Adam waiting for her. Sir had exited the jet and was walking towards the vehicle, waiting on the runway. Adam gave Brenda a polite head nod, and she returned it as she rushed to exit the vessel and catch up with Sir. An attendant opened the door to allow Sir to get in before popping the trunk and making his way back to the jet for their bags. Sir and Brenda were now in the rear seats, and everyone's belongings were loaded in the trunk. Adam got in the driver's seat, and they were on their way.

The café where they would eat breakfast was small with modern decor and an open concept that allowed the natural morning light to fill the room perfectly. As they sat to eat breakfast, Brenda couldn't help but feel the awkwardness of eating with Sir rather than waiting on him.

"Does this waitress know to set your utensils on your left side, or should I inform her?" Brenda joked as she browsed the menu.

"She knew before we landed. No need," Sir replied with a smirk. "The menu is not in English. Would you like me to clarify any items you may be interested in before she returns to take your order?"

"No. I already used Google translate to figure out what I want," Brenda playfully snapped back at Sir.

They ordered their food and ate quickly, not to let too much of the day escape, before heading to the hotel and preparing for the first of five site visits on the agenda for Lisbon.

Brenda was pleased to learn that the breakfast café was within walking distance of the hotel. She would have the opportunity to really take in the beauty of the details in the stone works of the city. Brenda, in awe with every step, made her way to the hotel. The classic architecture and decorative stoned streets were more captivating than any pictures Brenda had seen on the internet during her research for the trip.

They approached the entryway of tall, dramatic, solid-wood doors. Adam pushed them open to be greeted by a doorman with a welcoming gesture, inviting them into the thoughtfully lit lobby. The greenery lining the walls and accenting every corner added to the classic appeal of the hotel. Sir stopped and turned to Brenda as he motioned Adam to continue to the front desk.

"What about this building stands out to you as a concept that could be integrated into modern Western urban architecture?" Sir inquired of Brenda.

"The first thing is the upward build of the structure, which allows one to take advantage of the air space the property offers. In more densely populated areas, this is still the most effective way to maximize square footage. The other thing is the extremely well-planned natural lighting. This building has an immense amount of decorative greenery complimented by the sunlight. I would take that same space and use it for food production. Whether residential or commercial, with proper horticulture planning, the grow spaces could be aesthetically pleasing and support the fresh produce needs of residents or a restaurant." Brenda excitedly answered as she continued to look around, taking in the details of the building.

Before the conversation could continue, Adam returned with three room keys.

"This way," Adam said, leading the way to their rooms.

Every detail of the building had been attended to. The crown molding complimented the style of the vases lining the hallways every ten feet. The drapes seamlessly flowed and fit the windows like a dress on a woman's body. A few more steps and Adam stopped at the door on his left.

"Your room," he said as he opened the door and handed Sir the key card.

"Thank you. I will see you both in one hour," Sir thanked Adam and confirmed his request with a head nod from both Adam and

Brenda before retiring to his room.

"This is your room," Adam informed Brenda as they took a few short steps to the next door. "I will be across the hall in that room should you need anything," Adam pointed before handing Brenda her key card and retiring to his room.

As soon as the door was completely shut, Brenda covered her mouth in rags-to-riches awe at the setup of her mini apartment. There was a hallway in this hotel room. It was officially a higher class than anything she had ever stayed in. She ran around the floor plan in excitement and gasped when she stumbled into the marble wonder of this suite used as a bathroom. She immediately turned on the water to fill the bathtub. One hour was all she had to get this excitement out and do the bougiest things she could think of. Running back into the bedroom of her suite, she noticed that her bags had been placed on her bed. Perfect. She unpacked as the tub filled with steaming hot water and half a bottle of bubbles.- With her outfit for the day laid across the bed, Brenda stripped down as she grabbed a wine glass from the bar area adjacent to the sleeping quarters. Not having a taste for alcohol or wine, she skipped over the stocked bar and grabbed an instant Kool-Aid pack from the side of her luggage along with one of the twelve-dollar bottles of water from the hotel refrigerator. A bubble bath in a marble tub while drinking Kool-Aid out of a wine glass was not too bad for her first few hours in Europe.

Refreshed and feeling ready to take on the day, Brenda looked over at the time as she twisted her untamed curls back into place. Three minutes to spare. She'll be ready early and wait in the hall for them, she thought as she grabbed her carrying case for work and her key card. Adjusting her dress as she opened her room door, she looked up in surprise to see Sir and Adam already in the hall.

"Glad you didn't make us have to knock on your door," Sir said as he and Adam turned to walk down towards the lobby.

Not having a witty response to her efforts of being early, actually being almost late, Brenda just followed in silent excitement for the agenda for the rest of the day. The Sé de Lisboa was first. Adam pulled up to the parking area several feet from the entrance to this thirteenth-century Roman Catholic cathedral. The age and personality of the architecture immediately took all of Brenda's attention.

"Brenda!" Sir roared after several attempts for her attention fell on distracted and deaf ears.

"Yes, Sir!" Brenda jumped as she turned, snapping back to reality.

"You have two hours to complete your assignment at this site. Adam will accompany you for safety. Please complete all your notes and written submissions by the end of the two hours," Sir said in his usual stern and still voice.

"Yes, Sir," Brenda acknowledged as she turned to rush to the entrance of the cathedral, notebook out and pen in hand.

Adam quickly followed behind Brenda as Sir went in the opposite direction. Slowing down as they reached the entrance steps, Brenda hopped up and down with anticipation at the line moving forward so they could enter this magnificently built structure.

"So tell me, what's really the deal with Sir? He got a real name? What's his real job? What's my real job? If y'all thinking about murdering me overseas, I already told my best friend y'all names, office addresses, and license plate tag numbers. You know, just to be safe," Brenda drilled Adam.

"You ask too many questions. Yes. Your boss. To look at these buildings and write stuff in that notepad. And you're still alive, so I think you're safe at this point," Adam matter-of-factly responded.

"Well, at least I know you can say more to me than a head nod," Brenda joked, making light of Adam's more relaxed disposition in the absence of Sir.

Adam dismissed her comment with a head nod, indicating the line was moving forward. Brenda moved forward and became childlike in awe as she took in the high ceilings and beautiful arches. She only had two hours to explore this magnificent place. Conversation with Adam could wait. She broke off into a speed walk that would have been a jog if she had gone a half step faster. Shooting to less crowded areas first, Brenda gazed and wrote and wrote and wrote some more. Adam's protective eye watched from a distance as a parent would look after a child at a park. She was in her element, and he wanted to give her space to get lost in her world. Three miles of circles walked around the building later, Adam came up behind Brenda and said, "It's almost time to go. You have fifteen minutes before we will head back outside."

"Okay. Thanks, Adam. I didn't even realize the time. We can sit here, and I'll finish my notes before we head out," Brenda said through an excited and bright smile. She continued, "You travel everywhere with Sir, right? So you've seen all these things before, huh?"

"I'm not with him at this exact moment, so that throws everywhere out, but I do tag along enough to be pretty well-traveled," Adam answered.

"This is my first time in Europe and seeing buildings like these. I'm fascinated and nervous at the same time. What kind of job pays me to sightsee, I don't know," Brenda laughed nervously, asserting her position of still having her suspicions about this whole employment arrangement.

"You are smart to be cautious, but your concerns are not valid. Sir is something like a stealth philanthropist. He enjoys empowering people through their passions, which he sees can be useful in his business model. You're not just sightseeing. Take your assignments and notes seriously. They are going to be key to your success in your role," Adam advised her. "Now stop talking so much, and let's go."

"Alright, alright," Brenda smiled and agreed as they made their way out of the cathedral.

As expected, Brenda saw Sir's tall and dominating frame walking toward the vehicle they had arrived in earlier—right on time. If they kept pace, both herself and Adam would reach the truck at nearly the exact same time as Sir. Punctuality at its creepiest.

"How did you do completing your assignment for this site, Brenda?" Sir greeted her.

"Excellent, Sir. The direct information needed was easy to obtain, and the character in this building gave me plenty of things to make notes on," Brenda answered with a smile.

"Good. We have two more sites on the agenda for today," Sir informed Brenda and then turned to Adam.

"Take us to Terreiro do Paco next, please," Sir instructed.

"Yes, Sir," Adam acknowledged as he pulled out of the parking space and headed to their destination.

They arrived at the square that was full of life, with people coming in and out of shops and restaurants. In the center of the court was a statue of a man riding a horse facing an opening of the square along the Tagus River. The yellow-painted stone against the orange-shingled roofs and the natural grey of the structure seemed lit up by the sun itself from the open side of the square. Again, Brenda was in awe. Eager to get to her assignment, she led the way as they walked to the courtyard. She turned to Sir and asked, "Two hours, right?"

"One. And we will have lunch here at the Terreiro do Paco at the end of that hour," Sir informed her and Adam as he motioned for her to begin exploring. Notepad and pen in hand, she and Adam were off.

The hour passed quickly. Brenda smiled as she spotted Adam walking towards her. He no doubt was informing her of the time.

"I know, it's time. And I already peeped the restaurant Sir mentioned, and it's five minutes that way. We have fifteen to spare. My notes are finished, and I'm ready," Brenda said proudly before Adam could form a word. A slight head nod and smirk were all Adam gave in response as he led the way to the restaurant. Checking in at the front, Brenda scanned the dining hall and noticed Sir already seated. The waitress motioned, and she and Adam followed the server to their table.

"How was your hour?" Sir began the conversation as they sat down.

"Wonderful!" Brenda said excitedly. "The functional use of this historic space is outstanding. I was able to go in and out of several shops, and the practical modifications made in each unit were well-planned, not negatively affecting the structure. I had the opportunity to get notes on several different architectural styles within this one structure," she finished.

"Glad to hear your hour was productive. Let me know if you need any assistance with translations for your order. We will not dine too long as we still have one more stop for today," Sir said before raising his menu, not to invite further conversation.

"Yes, Sir. And thank you. I've managed pretty well with Google Translate, but I'll let you know if I need any assistance," Brenda said softly.

Black rice and lamb were all that seemed appetizing on the adventurous menu of this restaurant. Octopus and several raw sushi options were alternatives she wasn't culturally ready to digest. After a short and conversationless meal, Sir took care of the bill, and they were off to their last destination.

"Adam, to Castelo de Sao Jorge," Sir instructed as they loaded into the truck.

"Yes, Sir," Adam said as he updated his GPS and prepared to pull off.

They arrived at the stoic, fairytale-like castle. Never having seen an actual castle before, Brenda gazed at the building sitting high on a hill, imagining soldiers standing at the helms of the entryway arches. A small piece of the world in which time stood still. In awe, Brenda turned to Sir, "Please say two hours."

"Yes. Two hours, and we will head back to the hotel," Sir affirmed.

Brenda was off, and Adam took off in a slight jog behind her to catch up. She was more difficult to keep an eye on than a child in this castle. Turning every corner, looking over, and climbing every wall, Brenda took notes of the smallest details. Getting close to time, Brenda approached Adam, "This building has been here hundreds of years. Just imagine the hurricanes, earthquakes, old-school cannon battles, and probably dragons this building has seen. The simplicity of the structure and limited knowledge and tools during that time, and still, here this building is, hundreds of years later. Fascinating."

"Yep. It's an old magic dragon building. Fascinating," Adam sarcastically responded. "Let's head back to the fairy entrance where the noels are waiting to ask us a riddle to get across the bridge to exit the castle."

Brenda let out a heartfelt laugh and led the way back to the castle's entrance.

"Great and productive day," Sir said with a sigh as Adam and Brenda approached the vehicle. "We will head back to the hotel, where you will go over your notes for the day and have final drafts ready for submission at dinner," said Sir.

"Sounds like a plan," Brenda responded as she climbed into the truck.

They arrived back at the hotel and retired to their rooms. Walking into her suite, Brenda noticed a fresh set of flowers had been placed in the vase at the end of the hallway, where the room opened up to the lounging quarters of the suite. Daily housekeeping—of course. She continued to the room to prepare to shower the activities of the day away when she noticed a garment bag hanging on the open door of the wardrobe closet. She pulled it down and opened it to see a beautiful blue evening gown. She went to lay it out on the bed to discover two boxes. One with shoes, and the other with earrings, a bracelet, and a necklace to compliment the dress.

Brenda held her head to the sky and closed her eyes. "Ohhhhhhh, this looks expensive enough to be rented! He definitely wants this ass! But I ain't gone give it to him, Lord. I'm here for a job, and that job is not tricking, God, so please suppress any hoe thoughts I may be having. I don't want to buss it open for a real one overseas. I want to pray and love my husband in the regular house he's going to buy me off of eighth street back home. I will not let this rented dress and jewelry set draw me into making any hoe decisions. In the name of Jesus, who called that hoe out at the well, for the holiness of my vagina and the maintenance of my dignity, I pray. Amen."

Not having time to waste to prepare for the obsessively punctual dinner with Sir and Adam, Brenda ran her bath water and grabbed her twelve-dollar bottle of water, Kool-Aid pack, and wine glass. She needed to wash the day away and relax her mind before reviewing her report. Fresh-faced and feeling renewed, Brenda sat in the lounging area of the suite in her bathrobe and reviewed her notes to compile her final report for the day. Brenda found it interesting to explore such old architecture and put thought into how many of these dated building techniques could serve a purpose in improving modern building concepts. She placed the folder with her report on the table and went to put on the stunning evening attire that was tempting her to be a hoe. "If I am gone be a hoe, at least I'm being an expensive hoe," she said to herself as she evaluated her curves in the mirror.

6
GIVE IT TO ME STRAIGHT

Knock Knock Knock Knock Knock... Knock Knock.

"Coming," Brenda said as she finished applying the final strokes of mascara to her eyelashes. Taking a deep breath, she opened the door, surprised to see Sir standing there in a suit.

"Am I late?" Brenda asked sarcastically.

"No. You came to the door dressed, so you're on time," Sir smirked as he extended his hand, giving Brenda an invitation to walk with him.

"Well, good," Brenda gave a soft laugh back.

"Do you have your report?" Sir asked in his usual stern and serious tone.

"Yes, Sir. Right here," Brenda replied as she grabbed the folder tucked under her arm for safekeeping.

"Well, good. The evening attire looks beautiful on you," Sir complimented Brenda as he gave a devilish smirk.

"Thank you! How much you rented all this for, just to see me in it, boss?" Brenda joked.

"I haven't rented anything since I was assigned a locker in high school. It's all yours," Sir said with authority as he led Brenda to dinner.

Again, at a loss for words, Brenda quietly followed along as Sir led her down the hallway. Almost to the end of the hall, Brenda noticed Adam was not with them.

"So, I brought my report. Is this dinner still on company time?" Brenda inquired as she looked back at Adam's door, expecting him to emerge.

"Yes, it is. For you," Sir responded. "Adam and I are off, but you're still working until your report for the day is submitted."

"Oh, okay. So, this is work for me, and off-the-clock report reviewing for you? Noted," Brenda said with a side eye as she realized it would be just the two of them for dinner.

Nerves began to creep up as she couldn't imagine how to balance his strong personality in this new setting without the friendly balance of Adam in the equation. Here was her chance to get to know more about Sir, first hand, and she was nervous. Would he be satisfied with the report? Would he be professional, or would he go straight to asking for ass over bread and butter? With no idea of what to expect, and without the clear restraint provided in Adam's presence as a safeguard, this would be an interesting exchange. They exited the hotel to a black car waiting out front with a chauffeur standing next to the open door.

"Sir. Madam," the chauffeur greeted them as they approached the car.

Sir helped Brenda in and followed behind her before thanking the chauffeur as he closed the door.

"I will read your report over dinner and give you immediate feedback. This is your first report to me, so if I am critical, know that it is to ensure proper expectations are set for any future reports," Sir said softly as they rode through the bumpy cobblestone streets.

"Understood," Brenda said softly.

They pulled up to Alma restaurant. The chauffeur exited and walked around the car to open the door on Sir's side. The light caught Brenda perfectly as she exited the vehicle. Her melanated skin against the vivid blue of her dress, and gold jewelry accenting her neckline, ears, and wrist, turned the heads of every gentleman in front of the restaurant. Sir took Brenda gently by the hand and they entered the restaurant where an attendant was there to escort them to their private seating area.

"So, how was your first full day?" Sir asked.

"Interesting, fun, educational, a lot of walking," Brenda answered excitedly.

"So, your report should be pretty detailed, gauging from the excitement in your voice," Sir smirked.

"I'm eager for you to review it. Tell me what you do and don't like. And be direct. Not that you wouldn't be," Brenda said, inviting Sir's criticism as she handed him the folder. "If you'll excuse me, I'm going to go to the powder room for a few moments, so I don't have to stare at you while you read," Brenda said as she got up to leave the table.

"Don't take too long. I'm a fast reader. I don't need much time," Sir obliged her request.

As Brenda walked away to the powder room, Sir took a moment to admire the dress he had wanted to see Brenda in. It served his imagination perfectly. All her curves were exactly where he had thought them to be. He took only a moment to admire how the dress framed her body before redirecting his attention to her report in his hands. It was incredibly detailed and thorough. All the required questions were answered, and there was not one section without additional optional feedback. Her passion for architecture was clear. Sir was satisfied with his choice of her for this position.

"You took too long," Sir said with a light sarcastic voice as Brenda returned to the table.

"You read too fast," Brenda playfully responded, relieved to observe his light mood after reviewing the report.

"Your passion for your work is evident in your report. I am pleased. I hope this is what I can expect regularly. Not just extra effort to impress on your first day," Sir praised Brenda.

"I'm glad you are pleased. I will always do my best and strive for better, so the bar is set. Feel free to call me out if you see me slacking," Brenda confidently addressed Sir.

"So, your report is good. Tell me about other things. It is obvious this is your first time in Europe. How are you enjoying the food, the weather?" Sir asked.

"It's all new and beautiful to me. I'm loving every moment. There is one thing that is the source of some anxiety… This is a pretty non-traditional, unorthodox employment arrangement and you're a pretty reserved and quiet guy. How exactly does this European tour serve a purpose for my job function? It's been twenty-four hours and I haven't been trafficked, so I'm over that fear, but I still can't understand what job or task I could complete that would justify the need for an architectural tour of Europe?" Brenda bluntly asked.

"It will make sense in due time. Just continue doing good work like this, and you'll be fine," Sir assured her.

Not satisfied with that answer but enjoying the more relaxed mood of Sir at that moment, Brenda elected not to continue to poke at the bear. She shifted the conversation to an equally interesting question she wanted answered.

"So, give it to me straight. Did you just give me this job to woo me, marry me, and steal the passion of my youth by getting me pregnant and obligating my life to raising your demanding and entitled children?" Brenda asked, looking Sir directly in his eyes.

"What?!" Sir responded in laughter, unable to contain himself. "You really think things through, don't you?"

"Yep. You're rich, have a penis, no wedding ring, and have employed a tenderoni, who you're having dinner with, off your clock, but on mine, in a dress that hugs my hips, grips my ass, and my titties sit in perfectly with no bra. Make it make sense to me, Sir. You either want me, or you're gay and want to confide in me to be your fake wife, and Adam is your secret lover. Those are the only possible explanations to this whole situation. Now, give it to me straight," Brenda demanded as she sipped on her sparkling water.

"Neither is the case. You are a beautiful young lady; I will not deny that. But I do not know you enough to want you. I want your passion for architecture to be an engine in my projects where I see fit. If I see other passions that I want, you'll know," Sir said as he lifted his hands giving a welcoming gesture to servers. "Ah, perfect timing. The food is here. I ordered for you during your extended break on the clock in the powder room," Sir joked as the servers set the table.

"And you're ordering my food for me like we go together. Okay, Mr. straight, uninterested, you like my passion, Sir. I'm going to eat this food like it's my job since this is work. No need to be cute and not scrape the plate," Brenda said as she proceeded to indulge in all the new foreign flavors in front of her.

"Enjoy. You're almost off the clock," Sir ended their exchange.

They ate the rest of their meal in silence, giving only word to the servers of affirmation that the food was acceptable. The check came, Sir paid, and they left the restaurant to be escorted back to the hotel by the same chauffeur. Reaching the hallway of their rooms, Sir politely dismissed himself at Brenda's door, not making any inappropriate advances.

"Have a good evening, Brenda. Get you some rest as tomorrow will be assignments as well as traveling," Sir said softly, turning to retire to his own room before Brenda opened her door.

"Thank you, Sir. Have a good evening," Brenda nodded as she pulled out her key card to enter her room.

First complete day down and Brenda was still alive. She carefully placed her new dress back in the garment bag and the shoes and jewelry back in their respective boxes. In her nightshirt, she knelt next to her bed and bowed her head.

"Dear God, this man's pimp hand is strong. He did not disrespect me or make any aggressive advances at me the whole night. But he did buy this dress just to see me in it, Lord. If his intentions were holy, he would have bought me an abaya and hijab. But he rich, God, and could have his pick of women, so why me? If he is Adam's bottom, please reveal it, Lord. I can be a rich man's trophy, but a gay man's front is not in my portion. Thank you, God, for not letting me get trafficked and allowing me to get paid to do this ethically questionable job. If I end up having to smuggle drugs back into the country, God, please let them wrap me in it and not make me swallow it. I do not want to die like those Colombians in that movie whose stomach acid ate through the bags en route to America. Is there cocaine in Europe, God? If it's just weed, I think I'll be okay. Just make them lose the drugs altogether and keep me safe, God. In Jesus' name. Amen."

Ring! Ring! Ring!

Brenda jumped up, startled by the loud bell of the old telegraphic phone.

"This is your morning wake-up call. Breakfast will be delivered to your room shortly, and you will be set for departure in an hour and a half," a polite female voice advised.

"Thank you," Brenda forced out through the rasp of her morning voice.

Before she could rest her feet in the hotel-provided room slippers, there was a loud *Knock Knock Knock* at the door.

"Room Service," the attendant announced in his thick Portuguese accent.

"Coming!" Brenda shouted as she cloaked herself in her bathrobe and rushed to the door.

Fresh fruit, boiled eggs, several delicious-looking unidentified dishes, and a pot of black coffee with cream and sugar on the side rolled   into   the   room. "Thank you so much," Brenda said as the attendant backed out of the room with a polite gesture.

Brenda tasted a little bit of everything, just for the experience. She had to have something to go back home and say she ate to make her cultured. She was open to every new experience this job was offering.

Fresh out of the shower, Brenda decided to pack her belongings before leaving the room for the day's assignment. Today she would be traveling to Madrid and did not want to have to rush her assignments to come back to the room to pack.

An hour and twenty minutes after the wake-up call, Brenda emerged from her room only to see Adam had beaten her to the hallway this morning.

"Good morning, Adam," Brenda greeted him with a bright and rested smile.

"Good morning, Brenda. I hope you are rested and ready for the day," Adam said, returning a half smile.

"I am. And I packed already so whenever it's time to leave, I just can grab everything and go," Brenda informed Adam.

Just as Brenda finished speaking, Sir emerged from his room.

"Good morning. I see Brenda is doing much better with time already," Sir smirked as he greeted them.

"Yes, Sir. And she was just telling me that she has already packed her belongings for travel later today," Adam responded.

"Good," said Sir. "I expect that breakfast was acceptable for you both?" Sir asked.

"Yes," Adam said short and directly.

"I'm not sure what most of it was, but it was good," Brenda smiled as she expressed her excitement for her new breakfast experience.

"Good. Let's not waste any time as we have two sites to visit before departure today," Sir urged as he started towards the lobby of the hotel.

Everyone loaded into the truck; Brenda was bright-eyed and ready for a new day of assignments.

"Let's go to Oriente Station first, Adam," Sir instructed.

"Yes, Sir," Adam said as he pulled off to take them to their destination.

They arrived and Brenda stepped out of the truck and stood frozen for several moments. This was a modern marvel that gave all the dramatic lines of the centuries-old structures she had seen yesterday. It was as if the building was a loading dock for spaceships. So artistically built, Brenda immediately began to take notes of how the structure's design was possible. So many angles and arches, straight lines, and curves all in one structure.

"One hour," Sir said, giving a wave to Brenda that she could go and no longer had to stand there pretending as if she wasn't about to break out into a full run towards the building.

Adam followed behind her at a distance and allowed her to be free in her element. He watched as she oohed and awed at the unique design before her, taking notes in her pad at every step.

"Fifteen minutes," Adam said softly as he walked up behind her.

"Thank you," Brenda said as she turned to acknowledge Adam's presence. She had completely forgotten anyone was there or that she was on a schedule. "Give me a minute, please? Brenda asked. "I want to sit here and update a few notes before we head back that way."

"Take your time. You have fifteen," Adam said politely.

"So, how come you weren't at dinner last night?" Brenda asked curiously as she scribbled in her notepad.

"Because I was off. Is last night's dinner in your notes for today's assignment?" Adam asked.

"Yeah. One of the beams over there reminded me of the shape of a wine glass I saw last night. Have to make sure I note everything," Brenda sarcastically responded. "So, you know I asked your boss did he want me?" Brenda said, making eye contact with Adam so he knew the seriousness of her statement despite her jovial tone.

"Well, that should have been interesting," Adam responded. "Come on, your time is almost up, and you seem to be done with your notes," he continued, dismissing the invitation for further discussion on the topic.

"Don't you want to know what he said?" Brenda asked as she followed behind Adam, who was not walking towards the front of the station.

"Not really, but I'm guessing you're going to tell me anyway," Adam exhaled as he heard the next sentence coming from Brenda even before she spoke.

"You're such a good guesser. So, he said he didn't know me enough to want me. Then I told him he was either playing himself or you were his gay lover and y'all both are trying to use me as a front," Brenda explained.

"What?!" Adam said, turning around in shock at Brenda's statement. "You did not say that," Adam argued.

"And you didn't say y'all aren't lovers! Ha! Knew it!" Brenda said as she clapped her hands confidently, self-assured.

Adam laughed, "Definitely not lovers. Neither of us are gay for starters. And if he said he has not known you enough to want you, he's being honest. He has employed you because of your passion. I can see it in how you get lost in these buildings. Take that at face value, and any other assumptions you have with a grain of salt."

"Sooooo, you're not his bottom?" Brenda followed up.

"Say something stupid again, and I'm going to let you get lost and kidnapped out here," Adam said plainly, obviously not amused by Brenda's persistence.

"Okay, okay, so y'all are not gay. Then he wants me and is trying to kill my dreams, make me his trophy, and force me to bear and raise five of his entitled children," Brenda assured Adam.

"You're wrong there too," Adam laughed.

"I can't be too off. Rich guy, young, amazingly attractive, brilliant, lively, stylish, bold…"

"Are you done?" Adam interrupted.

"…No… adventurous, ambitious, and let's not forget sweet. How could he not want me? Plus he bought me this Boom Bam Bow dress to wear to dinner last night. It's obvious," Brenda said confidently.

"Just focus on your job and you might make it home alive. Turn in a bad report and he might traffic you," Adam laughed as he taunted Brenda.

"See, now that ain't even funny. I been sharing my location with my best friend this entire trip. She know where we at right now," Brenda said nervously.

They ended their playful conversation as they approached the truck, in sync with Sir.

"All set to head to Pavilhao de Portugal?" Sir asked, helping Brenda into the truck.

"Yes, Sir," Brenda affirmed as she placed her notepad and pen in her carrier for the ride.

"Adam, let's go. If we stay on schedule we should have time for lunch before departure," Sir said.

"Yes, Sir," Adam said as he pulled off to head to their final site in Lisbon.

Simple and still stunning, Brenda was in awe at the structure even from a distance. How such stonework, seeming to defy physics, stood so beautifully, she was eager to understand. This was again, a modern piece of architecture that was in contrast to the buildings she had observed the day before. The grandeur of the large, single-slab stone that served as the focal point of the structure was the first thing noted in Brenda's pad.

"One hour?" Brenda asked before the truck even came to a complete stop.

"One hour," Sir confirmed with a slight smile at her excitement.

Brenda jumped out of the truck before Adam even turned the engine off.

"She'll be back in one hour," Adam assured Sir as he jumped out to follow the eager Brenda, already halfway to the wall of the structure.

Brenda lost herself in her love for what her eyes had never seen. She was no less fascinated at this site as she had been at all the others. The hour flew by, and down to the minute, Brenda wrote in her notepad about this structure. Being mindful of commute time and the departing flight they had to catch, they loaded the truck and Adam suggested, "Sir, I can stop at the hotel and load the truck so the commute from lunch can be directly to the jet, if that is acceptable to you?"

"That will be fine, Adam. I'll call ahead and be sure we are ready to be seated when we arrive," Sir confirmed.

Brenda sat in the back seat, oblivious to the conversation taking place around her. She was intently going through her notes and already preparing her report for the day. Sir was pleased to observe her commitment to the work and did not disturb her focus as they traveled to the hotel and restaurant for lunch.

The lunch café was quaint with a limited menu. The servers were polite, and the food was served quickly. They ate and headed to the airport twenty minutes ahead of schedule. Madrid, and then Paris. Brenda was ready to explore it all.

7
OKAY SIR, WHAT'S YOUR GAME?

They landed in Madrid in the evening hour, just before sunset. The schedule for the rest of the day was to check into their rooms and prepare for dinner to provide the day's report. Brenda walked into her room, lovely as expected, to see an evening dress laid across the bed. "New dress for dinner every night?" Brenda questioned as she held the dress up to evaluate it.

"Yeah, this is definitely going to hug me," she laughed to herself as she imagined Sir browsing dresses for the perfect one. He had impeccable taste though. Accepting Adam's advice to just stay focused on doing her job well, Brenda reviewed her report and updated it to her satisfaction before getting dressed and heading to the door for dinner. She opened the door just as Sir raised his hand to knock.

"I'm ready," Brenda smiled as she watched Sir admire her in her new evening attire.

"You look lovely," Sir said as he extended his hand to lead her to dinner.

The dinner was uneventful and awkward. Sir, again, was satisfied with the report, and with no conversation or negative feedback to discuss her work, Brenda was at a loss for how to handle this "on-the-clock" dinner conversation. She did not want to make the mistake of being too forward. She had already told this man what he wanted and that he was possibly gay at the first dinner. Push the issue any further, and it was going over a cliff. They ate and Sir communicated sparsely to ensure she was satisfied with the food, and they retired back to the hotel. Sir delivered Brenda to her room respectfully, making no advances. That following morning, just as in Lisbon, the first sites they visited in Madrid were historic sites, with centuries-old architecture. Brenda explored as Adam escorted her to ensure she did not run into any trees while she looked up at buildings and back down at her notepad. A full day later, Brenda retired to her room to slip into her routine of preparing a report and putting on a new dress for dinner with Sir.

Tonight's dress was exceptionally modest. It was very fitted but very covered up. Satisfied with Sir's selection, Brenda got dressed and greeted Sir in the hallway as he walked towards her room.

"I don't think there is a style of dress that is unflattering on you," Sir complimented Brenda.

"Thank you," she blushed as she turned to model the dress for Sir. "It helps that you have good taste."

Sir sipped a glass of wine as their food arrived and asked for Brenda's report. As he was reviewing it, Brenda grew nervous, not being able to discern his facial expressions. Was he surprised or dissatisfied?

"Brenda," he called her attention.

"Yes," she cautiously answered.

"Your reports are improving. The information is much more organized and concise. Good job," Sir said to her in a flat, disinterested tone.

"Thank you, Sir. I'll continue to do my best to continually improve," Brenda replied.

"I appreciate your passion and commitment. We have a very early flight in the morning, so we will not make this dinner long. Let me know when you are satisfied, and we can go," Sir said.

"I'm full. I'm ready whenever you are," Brenda said.

They retired to their rooms, as always, Sir on a respectful note.

It was well before sunrise, and Brenda was already up and waiting at the door with her bags. They would be on their way to Paris, the last stop on the European tour. *Knock knock knock!* Brenda opened the door and handed her bags to the bellhop to place on the cart beside him. She peeked around the doorway to see Sir and Adam standing in the hallway, ready to go.

"Good morning!" Brenda said excitedly.

"Well, you're wide awake pretty early," Sir said as he motioned to the bellhop that they were ready to load the bags.

"Yes, Sir! Ready for Paris. Can't wait to marvel at the Eiffel Tower!" Brenda confessed as she followed them down the hallway towards the lobby.

"It is beautiful and worth all of your marveling," Sir said as he continued through the long hallway to the lobby.

They arrived at the airport and took advantage of the complimentary coffee as the pilot readied the jet for takeoff. Bags loaded, and an attendant came several minutes later and addressed Sir, "Your vessel is ready to depart."

"Thank you," Sir replied and stood up with a quick motion for Adam and Brenda to head to the jet.

During the short flight, Sir and Adam napped in the still, dark morning sky. Brenda sat up, soaking up every bittersweet moment of the last leg of this trip. She had the most enjoyable time of her life and was on the clock getting paid to do it all. She could not even imagine this opportunity two weeks ago, bussing tables in the diner, hoping her degree would be worthwhile and pay for itself. The city lights of Paris dimmed against the sun as they made their descent into the city. It was beautiful.

Anxious to explore the city, Brenda inquired of Sir what the schedule was for the day.

"Breakfast, check-in, then your first assignment," Sir explained to her.

"Can we do a quick breakfast, like some coffee and a bagel? I'm wide awake and ready to get moving," Brenda begged excitedly.

"That will be fine," Sir told her.

They picked up some bagels and coffee en route to the hotel to satisfy Brenda's excitement. They pulled up to the hotel and Adam signaled for the bellhop to come and collect their bags.

"If no one has a pressing need to go to their rooms, I can have our belongings delivered, and we can head to our first site for today," Adam offered.

Brenda looked over at Sir in anticipation for his response. "That would work great. We can get some extra sightseeing in if we finish a bit early," Sir said.

"Yessssss!" Brenda exclaimed in excitement.

They were on their way to explore. Brenda had just under two days to see Cathédrale Notre-Dame de Paris, Palace of Versailles, Champs-Elysees, Sacre-Coeur, Montmartre, Musee d'Orsay, Louvre Museum, and of course the Eiffel Tower. She did not want to waste any time at the hotel. They reached their first stop, and before Brenda asked or was even given a time, she ran to the door.

"Come and find me in time!" she playfully yelled back to Adam as he was just closing the door of the truck to follow her.

"Slow down!" Adam said, catching up with Brenda. "You'll get kidnapped and trafficked for real in these Paris streets. Stay close and be attentive here," Adam advised Brenda.

Brenda took in Adam's instruction and made sure to stay close as they went from site to site and she compiled notes for her report for the day. Stopping only briefly to eat a baguette and some tea, Brenda was running off of pure adrenalin. Having visited five of the nine planned sites in Pairs, they retired to the hotel for the first time since they had arrived. Brenda was exhausted but altogether too excited to sit still. She immediately began polishing her report and took a shower before even opening the garment bag laying across her bed. She knew the dress would be beautiful.

The sweat of the day now off of her, Brenda gasped and dropped her towel as she unzipped the garment bag. The dress was stunning. More revealing than she might have chosen, but nonetheless stunning. They could not just be going to dinner with this dress. She snapped out of her trance of admiration and got dressed. Just as she was grabbing her report off the coffee table, there was a rhythmic knock on the door. It was Sir.

"I'm just a little bit late, but this dress was a little complicated to put on. I could not figure out where the rest of it was," Brenda joked as she opened the door.

"I should have bought less of it," Sir said with a devilish grin as he looked Brenda up and down. "I'm taking you to a ballet tonight before dinner. Let's go."

"I knew this dress was too fancy for food!" Brenda exclaimed with excitement as she turned to close her room door.

Yet another first on this trip, Brenda was jittery and bubbling over being able to see a professional ballet company perform. How much more perfect could this job get? She sat in the balcony booth of the theater, feeling through the story the dancers were telling. The opera singers performed in French, but the conviction and the universal language of music conveyed the story perfectly well. Sir looked over at Brenda in appreciation for her openness to the fine arts. She was young. He was surprised at her genuine attentiveness and interest in the performance. As the show came to an end, Brenda followed the room and stood to give the performers a standing ovation.

"I'm glad you enjoyed the show. We must go now if we are going to make our dinner reservations," Sir said as he gently took hold of Brenda's hand to guide her to the exit.

The chauffeur greeted them at the exit of the theater with the door of the car already open. "Right this way ,sir," he acknowledged the haste in Sir's movement as he quickly closed the door and got into the driver's seat. They traveled through the bustle of the busy night city, and Brenda looked out in awe at the beauty of Paris at night. There were so many lights accenting the dramatic buildings, highlighting the carved details of every stone. They reached their destination. L'Oiseau Blanc. A rooftop restaurant with a breathtaking view.

"Paris is beautiful," Sir said as he looked directly at the inattentive Brenda.

"It is!" she gasped in reply as she marveled at the skyline and the backdrop of the few visible stars in the cloudy night sky.

Brenda turned in surprise at Sir's deep stare, not blinking, of admiration. Joking her way through her blushing, Brenda gave a soft smile and said, "I must be as beautiful as Paris the way you're sitting over there staring."

"You are," Sir said without hesitation.

Brenda's blush forced her silence, and she masked her shy smile with a sip of wine.

The server came, and Sir ordered their dinner, as usual, as he returned his silent attention to Brenda. She felt his stares. His eyes were touching her body, but the wine was also touching her blood. Not to confuse how she was reading the stares and make an irredeemable mistake, Brenda broke the silence and placed the day's report on his side of the table. She wanted Sir to look at anything but her.

"Here is my report. I was unaware of the ballet, and I know it was on paid time, so I took some notes on a napkin that I can add to the report for tomorrow on the structure and details of the theater." Brenda said as she looked away into the view of the city, too nervous to see Sir's response.

"That won't be necessary," Sir smiled as he noticed her lack of strength to even look at him.

Hearing the smile in his voice, Brenda reflexively turned to look at

Sir. Expecting to see him reviewing the report, she fell into a lock of eyes with the stare that Sir had never broken.

"So, you finally looked at me," Sir laughed as leaned back, enjoying Brenda's flustered state. Once he was sure Brenda was watching him watch her, he shifted his eyes to appreciate the dress he had chosen for the night. He smiled at the soft print of her nipples in the dress. Brenda looked down and noticed her body had given her away. Shifting her position, she awkwardly hid her erect nipples with her forearms and reached for a lifeline, "Are you finally going to look at the report?"

"I will look at what I want to look at when I want to look at it. I'm appreciating what's in front of me, and based on what I see, you want me to see what I'm looking at," Sir said in a monotone voice with an intent gaze now redirected at Brenda's eyes.

Brenda's back straightened as her pelvic muscles tightened and the tickle of her swollen clit hardened her nipples even more. She was shocked at how clear and open Sir was being. If ever she was going to find out what Sir really wanted from her, this was the time to do it. Taking another sip of wine for courage, Brenda moved her arms to give Sir clear view of what he wanted and said ,"Okay Sir. What's your game? You're not trafficking me, you don't know me to want me, and you're not gay but you're worried about my hard nipples. Why?"

"I'm not worried about them. Just noticing you are excited," Sir smiled calmly.

Frustrated with the brick wall of Sir, Brenda decided she was either going to know what he wanted or call him on his bluff.

"The hour is getting late and if you're not going to review the report now, I would request that I could receive the feedback in the morning," Brenda said.

"Ready to get back to the hotel already? Have you forgotten that you haven't eaten yet?" Sir replied with a smile, amused at her eagerness.

"I've actually gotten full from the bread and the wine. It's been a long day," Brenda gently asserted.

"Okay. I'll have the food delivered to the hotel," Sir said as he signaled for the waiter.

They left the restaurant and took the short ride to the hotel in silence. When they arrived, Sir helped Brenda out of the vehicle and walked her to her room, as Brenda shyly avoided eye contact. Inserting her key card into the door, she turned and looked up to Sir's eyes. She gently touched his hand, giving him approval before she turned to enter her room, leaving the door wide open behind her. Sir walked in and locked the door.

The city lights peeping through the windows created glimmering shadows on Brenda's dress. She walked into the bedroom suite and removed her earrings. As she sat her second earring on the nightstand, she jumped with the surprise of Sir's hand touching her shoulder. He ran his fingers down her arm and back up again before continuing his journey to her neck. Tracing her collar bone to the strap of her dress. Sir pulled Brenda's short framed into his with the softness of her butt pillowing his growing manhood. He followed the line of the dress to her breast with his fingers outlining her shape before palming her warm, firm bosom, pulling her in closer into his growing erection. Brenda placed her hand on his and gently tugged for him to release her. He let go and she turned around. Taking a few steps toward the garment cabinet, Brenda removed her dress and lowered her eyes as she presented all of herself to Sir. She walked towards him and reached out to feel his approval. His erection was rock hard.

Confirmed in his satisfaction with her so far, Brenda guided Sir to the bed and removed his Blazer before undressing his lower half. She bent down in front of him and gave a soft kiss to the head of his pleasure. Sir withdrew his hands to his side giving Brenda permission to continue. She squatted down in front of him, using his thigh as support with one hand, and the grip on his dick to balance with the other, she swayed as she licked him from base to tip. She studied and tasted him with her mouth, following his maze of veins with her tongue. Having mapped out his muscle, Brenda licked her lips before swallowing as much of him as she could. Sucking his veins with her tongue, she stroked back and forth until Sir grabbed her hand on his thigh and said "Enough of that. Stand up."

Brenda stood, and Sir turned to guide her to the bed and laid her on her back. He opened her legs to examine her. The sight of her small, moistened flower made him grunt as he joined her in the bed. He placed his hands on her inner thighs and pinned her legs open with his weight before positioning the head of his penis at the opening of her love. Leaning into her embrace, Sir kissed Brenda as he rested his chest against hers. He increased the pressure. Brenda moaned as he massaged her clit with the slips of his pressure. Finding his angle, Brenda pushed at Sir's shoulders as he strengthened his stroke, determined to penetrate her. Her thighs were pinned open, and his body held hers in place as she pushed his shoulders harder and harder in attempts to combat the pressure. He was going to have to ease into her. Having enough of the tip of himself inside of her, he released her thighs and lifted his chest from hers. Taking her hands into his and positioning them above her head, he increased the pressure. Her reflexes restrained with her hands secured above her head, he dove deeper into her pelvis as her back arched. His deep, strong strokes increased in tempo as he felt the cream of her throbbing coat him. He could no longer restrain her hands. He kissed her hard, releasing her hands to cuff both of her lower cheeks and hold her steady. Brenda hugged his shoulders with her freed hands bracing herself for his climax. He thrusted harder, going deeper, his tempo increasing with every yell. Brenda released as he bruised her moist walls. He hugged her tight as he froze in the depth of his penetration to feel his throbbing within hers.

8

GOD, YOU STILL SAVING HOES?

Brenda awoke to the loud ring of the hotel telephone.

"Good morning. Your breakfast will arrive in your room shortly, and the concierge will collect your belongings to transport you to the airport in two hours," said the attendant.

"Thank you," Brenda sleepily replied as she heard the knock of room service at the door.

"Coming!" Brenda exclaimed as she hung up the phone.

Naked and guilty, Brenda jumped out of the empty bed to put on a robe and answer the door. She opened it to her breakfast cart and Sir.

"You were still asleep," Sir grinned as he rolled her breakfast into the room. "Your report was thorough. Good job. I'll see you shortly to head out to the airport," he said as he stepped back out of the room.

"Thank you. I'll see you shortly," Brenda yawned through her blush.

Spending forty-five minutes of the two hours she had to get ready in a steaming shower, Brenda hastened to pack and organize her things. The knock at the door came just as she zipped up her last luggage.

"Good morning," Brenda smiled at the concierge as she rolled her luggage to be loaded onto the cart.

"Good morning," he politely returned her smile.

Taking a deep breath and checking herself in the body mirror adjacent to the door, Brenda put on her everything's normal and she did not just give a man some ass face before stepping into the hallway.

"Good morning!" She said excitedly before turning to an empty hallway. Her face dropped as the bellhop raised his head to see the ghost she was greeting. The sound of a hotel door opening a few moments later broke the silence of the awkward stare that followed. Adam exited his room into the hallway.

"Good morning!" Brenda repeated as she directed her focus to Adam.

"Good morning!" Adam sarcastically returned her excitement as he noticed the awkwardness between her and the bellhop.

"Good morning, sir," he acknowledged the bellhop. A few short moments later Sir emerged from his room.

"Good morning," he greeted the group. Their collective reply rang down the hallway as the last bags were loaded onto the cart, and they began towards the exit of the hotel. The journey was silent but not awkward. The bags were loaded and Brenda gazed out the window at the city streets as she waited for Sir and Adam to join her in the vehicle.

"Your breakfast was satisfactory, I hope," Sir addressed Brenda as he stepped into the truck.

"It was," Brenda softly assured him.

"Good," Sir said before addressing Adam.

"I received confirmation of an on-time flight schedule for this morning. Go ahead and confirm my schedule in the states for tomorrow, today."

"Yes, Sir." Adam answered.

"And arrange for transportation for all of us to go home directly from the airport. Your break starts as soon as we land," Sir further directed Adam.

"Yes, Sir. Thank you, Sir," Adam nodded.

"Thank you," Sir replied as he turned on his tablet to review his schedule for the next day.

The morning bustle of the city lengthened the short ride to the airport and allowed Brenda to savor the smell and taste of the European air. Sir would steal short glimpses of her as she obliviously looked out of the lowered window with a bittersweet smile below her squinted eyes, desiring to see even the wind that rushed her face. They came to a stop at the entrance to the airport.

"If I say I left something, and we have to go back and miss our flight and have to stay another day, does it come out of my paycheck?" Brenda playfully inquired of Sir.

"Yes. Jet fuel, reservations, meals, and Adam's election of double or triple rate for services on off days," Sir plainly replied.

"Adam. Is tomorrow feeling like a double or triple day if you have to work?" Sir asked.

"Definitely a triple Sir. I would have to find someone to keep my goldfish another day and you know how expensive that can be," Adam supportively answered.

"Goldfish?! You can get four times your rate if you would like. I know how hard good goldfish help is to find," Sir continued, not breaking his focus from his tablet.

"Thank you, Sir. I appreciate that," Adam said.

"I ain't leave nothing," Brenda bitterly interrupted their exchange.

They touched back down in the United States and Brenda stretched as she awoke to the sound of the pilot's voice.

"We have touched down safely. Please gather your belongings and let my attendant know if there is anything you need before exiting the vessel. Thank you for trusting me with your travels today."

"That was quick," Brenda yawned as she folded the blanket she had snuggled up with mid-flight.

"Not for the pilot," Sir said sternly as he encouraged Brenda to match his and Adam's rush to exit the jet.

Brenda picked up the pace and headed to the open door of the vessel. Three sedans were parked about fifty feet from the landing space, with chauffeurs standing beside them. Adam exited first, walking over to confirm each car's destinations as Sir stepped out to assist Brenda closely behind him.

"That's you," Adam informed Brenda as he walked back up pointing to the middle sedan.

"Okay. Thank you," Brenda nodded.

"Enjoy your time off. I'll see you in a few days," Sir shook Adam's hand as he relieved him.

Adam walked back to his vehicle, making it to the door just as the chauffeur closed the trunk. "Do I get a few days off?" Brenda turned to Sir.

"You're off tomorrow. Your schedule resumes at 9 a.m. in the office after that," Sir responded professionally.

"Yes, Sir," Brenda said as she walked to the open door of her vehicle with the chauffeur waiting to assist her.

She pulled up to her apartment and fumbled through her travel bag for her keys as the chauffeur unloaded her luggage. Just as the door opened, she cuffed the chain of the keys and pulled them from their forgotten pocket in her travel bag.

"You don't have to walk my bags up. I can manage from here," Brenda thanked the chauffeur as she tipped him.

"Yes ma'am. Thank you, ma'am," the gentleman said as he rolled her luggage onto the sidewalk, lifting the handles in position for her to take hold of.

"Have a good one," she smiled as she turned to retire to her apartment.

Walking into the door of her apartment, she took a deep breath. She had not lived there long enough for it to feel like home, and it was nice enough to feel like she was still on vacation. She carefully made her way through the meticulously-staged living spaces to the bedroom. She placed her luggage near the dresser in the same routine of the hotels she had been visiting for the last several days, and stretched out across the bed.

Brenda woke up to a flash of lightning in the stormy night sky. Jet lag had won, and her eyes stretched with her observation of the hour. She was wide awake in the middle of the night and couldn't sleep with the thoughts just running through her brain. "Am I his hoe now? Will I be required to wear dresses and no panties from now on? Does he want a wife? Did he skeet in me for real, for real? How is this shit really going to go?" Tiring herself with the whys, what ifs and maybes, Brenda slowed her mind and prayed.

"God, You still saving hoes? If so, I'm here. Amen."

8:57 a.m., Brenda walked into the office with her hair in a conservative bun, modest makeup, and a flattering pantsuit.

"Good morning. Today's schedule starts with a secondary review of your reports and planning for phase two of your assignment," Sir's voice greeted Brenda from behind.

"Good morning." She turned and paused to try and read Sir's mood. Picking up on nothing more than business as usual, Brenda smiled through her nerves, "Yes, Sir. I'm ready. I've prepared a summary and comparison of the reports for you to review this morning," Brenda said as she followed Sir down the hall to his office.

"Is it okay for me to close the door?" Sir asked as Brenda sat in the chair in front of his desk.

"Yes," Brenda confirmed as Sir stood in the doorway awaiting approval. He closed the door and sat at his desk, opening the folder to review the summary Brenda had prepared.

"So, you spent your off day working?" Sir smiled as he skimmed the first page.

"Yes, Sir. My sleeping pattern was off, so I forced myself to do something to keep me awake so I could be ready for work today," Brenda explained.

"I appreciate your effort," Sir said as he closed the folder and looked over at the uncharacteristically quiet Brenda.

"Is there something on your mind? You seem reserved?" Sir leaned into his question.

"You asked, so I'm answering," Brenda said, staring at Sir. let out a soft laugh, pleased at Brenda's expected emotion-filled response. "You done did me now, so how does this work? You trying to love me? Pimp me? Own me? What? I just need to know so I can understand what my job is and ain't," Brenda rambled.

"Doing you was off the clock, so I can assure you it has no bearing or is included in the scope of your job responsibilities," Sir smiled. "As far as loving, pimping, or owning you, I don't desire any of that," Sir said, stiffening his tone.

"So, what do you desire?" Brenda asked.

"It's not that simple," Sir said.

"Well, let's simplify it," Brenda spit out, not willing to be dodged on this question.

"Okay then," Sir smiled at her aggression.

"I have needs and too much money for a wife. I can employ you to be a person I trust to assist in professional spaces, and you can be available as you're comfortable to assist in personal spaces," Sir offered.

"Being that you have too much money for a wife, what assurance do I get for being personally available?" Brenda questioned him further.

"What do you want?" Sir asked with confidence and without hesitation.

"A house. In my name. Fully furnished. On five acres. With a pond. And porch. And a garden. And a tractor to cut the grass," Brenda listed as she thought of what all she could capitalize on in the moment.

"Is that it?" Sir asked.

"No. And I want a contract saying you'll give me a million dollars for every stretchmark I get if you get me pregnant. I saw it on a celebrity TV report once, so I know those contracts exist," Brenda concluded.

"I'll have the contract drafted right away and you'll receive notice of your property once it is secured," Sir laughed as he stood from his desk. Cautiously approaching Brenda, he grabbed her hand to assist her in standing.

"Now that you have your assurances and your clarification, I'm going to give you the rest of the day off, being that you spent yesterday working," Sir said as he breathed in the familiar smell of her perfume.

"Yes, Sir. I appreciate it," Brenda said slowly as she welcomed his hand around her waist pulling her into an embrace.

Sir hugged Brenda into his erection that had been growing since she started listing her demands for her personal time.

Admiring her neckline, he kissed her gently below her ear.

"You wore pants to make it harder for me. But that just means you have to take it from the back. Thank you," Sir whispered before he turned Brenda around to cushion his hard muscle in the softness of her full ass.

He felt her up and down, his hands remembering the map of her curves from their prior encounter.

"You're welcome," Brenda devilishly smiled as she lowered her pants and rested her chest on the top of the desk in front of her.

Sir looked and rubbed a few circles of admiration on Brenda's cheeks before steadying her with a grip to her waist. He applied pressure. Slowly he massaged his desires with the vibrations of her moans as he worked deeper into her tense center.

A year passed and Brenda was nearing the completion of her first assignment. Sir had put her in charge of the design of a new office building, and the final inspections were scheduled in a few days. Brenda sat at her desk, verifying all the orders for the decor team with an optimistic expectation that furniture could begin delivery in ten days.

"Hey."

"Hey," Brenda lifted her head to Adam's familiar voice.

"Still picking out curtains?" Adam asked.

"No. The interior decorator picked them out. I'm just approving and ordering them," Brenda jovially replied.

"I'm closing this out now. I'll be downstairs in fifteen," she continued, catching Adam's subtle hint to the time.

Adam opened the door as Brenda walked out of the building.

"Fifteen minutes ended eight minutes ago," Adam scolded Brenda.

"Well, the elevator took nine minutes to come," Brenda lied playfully.

She sat in the back seat alone shuffling through her folders as Adam started the forty-minute commute to the building site.

"How are you feeling today?" Adam asked Brenda gently as he looked for the opportunity to pull out into traffic.

"I'm good. Just want to make sure no one left a wrench in an outlet or something," Brenda stressfully sighed.

"You know wrenches would serve no purpose in putting together an outlet, right?" Adam teased her.

"I do now, so I'll cross outlet wrench check off my list," Brenda softly smiled in appreciation for his concern.

They had arrived at Brenda's baby. Her first building project. A cross of classical and modern European architecture, the carefully placed lights complimented the angles of the building beautifully against the early evening sky. They entered the building, and Brenda stood in the doorway to take in the details of the vast and empty lobby. Imagining how beautiful her building would be once dressed with all the finishings brought a smile to her face.

"And just like that, she's gone," Adam said as he snapped his fingers.

"I'm not gone. I'm just remembering," Brenda said as she walked over to the desk of the lobby.

"These are the inspection sheets for each room. I'll leave one in each area for the crew to do a follow-up check tomorrow behind my check tonight," Brenda spoke to herself out loud.

"It'll be fine," Adam assured Brenda as he looked at her stressed face.

"I remember when you saw that thing you built over there in that one building," Adam pointed as he joined her observations and remembering.

She smiled and turned to see what he was referencing.

"Oh, yeah! I remember that too. I think that was the day I asked if you were Sir's secret gay lover." They both laughed.

"Go do your inspecting for this floor and I'll be right here when you're ready for the next," Adam encouraged her.

"How about you walk around with me so I don't drive myself crazy nitpicking?" Brenda suggested.

"If it'll help you, sure," Adam agreed.

Each office suite had subtle inspirations from the various buildings Brenda had seen in Europe. Adam and Brenda went from suite to suite, floor to floor, reminiscing on the days that sourced the inspiration. They reached the final floor. The top floor had strong influences from Paris. As they exited the elevator, Brenda twirled in the opened foyer of the suite, laughing loud and enjoying the echo of her voice bouncing between the windows, walls, and floors.

"You really loved Paris, huh?" Adam asked with a sarcastic, bitter tone.

"Yes, I did," Brenda said sharply, picking up on the shift in Adam's tone.

"Paris is a sure bet," Adam continued with clear distaste.

"Sure bet?" Brenda asked with a confused face.

"Nothing," Adam said, attempting to clear his tone.

"Okay then," Brenda shrugged.

"So, a house huh?" Adam asked as he looked away to some of the details in the room.

"What?" Brenda asked in her guilty shame.

"And a garden? And a tractor?" Adam continued. "Does your short ass even know how to drive a tractor?" Adam laughed.

Seeing no point in lying about what Adam obviously knew, Brenda lowered her head in shame and asked, "How'd you know?"

Sir and Brenda had been good about keeping their personal dealings private. The weekly office rendezvous had stopped as Brenda's job responsibilities increased, but Sir and Brenda's relationship was good. He was satisfied, and she was kept.

"A house he started building about a year ago was just completed. It's to be deeded over to your name in a few weeks. He had me make the arrangements for you to go see it and sign the paperwork the other day." Adam gave a disappointed smile.

Bright-eyed and excited about the news but sensitive to Adam's tone and a little embarrassed, she defended herself, "Well, if I had to be a hoe, at least I wasn't a free one."

"A hoe?!" Adam's loud laugh echoed through the hall.

"You're far from that. Smart would be a better description," Adam comforted her.

"So, if you had a coochie ,you'd sell it too?!" Brenda joked.

"Of course. And I'd be better off than you cause I'd sell mine on the internet," Adam asserted.

They both laughed and paused as their eyes met.

"Don't mention it, but you'll be laying eyes on your house in a few weeks. Now finish this inspection so we can go," Adam smiled as he turned to wait by the elevator for her.

Blushing and bubbling, Brenda skipped through the building, inspecting the remainder of the final floor. Daydreaming about how much house her coochie had purchased her, she completed her sheets and headed to the elevator not to have Adam wait too long.

9
WHAT'S FUNNY?

It was the night before the grand opening. The building inspection had gone perfectly, the decor team was reliable, and everything was on schedule. Seventy percent of the suites were already occupied, and the grand opening event was a who's who of the city's business elite.

"The building is stunning. You spent my money well. And my accountant tells me I could start to see profits from my investment in twenty months if we can maintain a consistent eighty percent occupancy rate," Sir said as he sat on the reading chair in Brenda's room, drying his leg from the shower.

"Thank you," Brenda smiled as she walked across the room to bring Sir his lotion. "We're at seventy percent as of today. The entire acquisition team is on schedule for tomorrow, and a mandatory meeting is scheduled four hours after the event to compare information obtained from prospects," she reported as she turned to walk to the bed.

Sir grabbed her by the tie of her silk night gown to redirect her to his knee. She sat and smiled, suppressing the full extent of her emotion not to give away her knowledge of what's supposed to be a surprise.

"You're really happy," Sir noted as he examined her face.

"You're really happy too," Brenda responded as she positioned her hip against Sir's fully erect towel.

"How did you let two weeks go by and you not feel me?" Brenda questioned him as she stood up and guided Sirs hands to her nakedness underneath.

"I like how you feel when you miss me," Sir replied as he turned

Brenda's rear to his face and spread her feet with his.

"Have a seat," he said with soft authority.

"Yes, Sir," Brenda complied. Arching her back and bracing tightly on both arm rests, she moaned as the tip of his strength began to open her neglected flower.

"Sit all the way down," Sir requested as he pulled her closer around him.

Brenda let out a soft yell each time she bounced the back wall of her depths off the tip of his girth. She bounced and bounced until her juices snailed down around his exposed veins to the base of him.

"I said all the way down," Sir groaned as he pulled Brenda down until their thighs met.

Brenda's body stiffened and Sir stood up, lifting her, holding himself inside of her. He walked her over to the bed where he gave her only a few moments of relief, removing himself to turn her over and quickly reinsert all of himself into her puddling pink center. Sir raced with the momentum causing her breast to bounce sharply with his every thrust. His pelvis met hers with every down on the bounce of Brenda's breast. Then two hits before the down. Now they're bouncing off beat. Three hits before the down. Now they're going in circles. Sir watched the circles her nipples drew, listening to the stuttering moans from her chest, feeling the trembling of her thighs, until he couldn't take it anymore and froze with all of his weight pushing into her center.

The grand opening was a two-hour event, giving an exclusive tour of the upscale business suites to prospective clients. Brenda's assignment was complete and today was the day that the opinions would fly. The business of it all was not Brenda's job, but she wondered, what would they say as they walked around the building? Would they notice all the details put into the corners? Should I wait to tell them a woman built this building until after I hear what they say? Overthinking and being self-critical, Brenda nervously twitched as she sat behind the closed doors of the reception hall, peeping at the arriving guests.

"You know you don't have to be here, right?" Sir snuck up behind a peeping Brenda.

"This building is built. The people will comment on the architecture, but they're really here about business. I can have someone else do the tour and give you a report of all the nice comments people said." Sir said, offering Brenda an escape from her nerves.

"Someone else tour the building I built?" Brenda objected with an eye roll.

"You just rolled your eyes at me," Sir said with sarcastic shock. "You're stressed. How about this? There's a late meeting on your schedule this evening. Go with Adam and tell him I said you can prepare for the meeting early, and I'll meet you later with feedback from our guests?" Sir threw her another lifeline. Brenda immediately knew this had to be about the house. She paused to formulate a way to agree to this without giving away her excitement.

"You sure?" was all Brenda could come up with.

"I'm sure," Sir said, suspicious of her lack of further objection.

"Okay. I think you're right. I'm stressed. I'll sit this one out," Brenda let out with a halfhearted, disingenuous sigh of disappointment. She turned and walked away slowly, looking as stressed and as disappointed as she could present her sheer joy to be. The door closing behind her, Brenda came out of character and burst into a sprint as she ran towards the truck to Adam. Seeing an empty parked vehicle, Brenda scanned the front outside area of the building for Adam's tall frame. There he was. "Excuse me," Brenda approached Adam as he spoke with security personnel.

"Yes," Adam turned to see her signaling the man he was speaking with to give them a moment.

"Sir said I don't need to do the tour; you can take me to my evening meeting early," Brenda jittered out with a quick breath and hop of excitement.

"Calm down. You don't even know what the meeting is for," Adam laughed and reminded her. "Now go wait by the truck and look sad that you're not doing the tour," he instructed her as he walked away to find Sir and inform him of their departure.

"How far away is it?! What color is it?! How big is the garden?" Brenda badgered Adam as soon as he merged onto the highway, and she was certain they were on their way with no need for any emergency turn around.

"It's not far. Just relax. You'll see it when you get there," Adam said.

About thirty minutes outside the city, they pulled up to a dirt road with decorative columns creating an entryway to a tunnel of trees. Driving for about two minutes in the shade of the canopy created by the trees, the sun blinded Brenda as it rushed through the window from behind the beautiful estate in front of them. The porch wrapped around half the front and side of the house. The paved entry way from the side porch split off to a paved path leading to a garden, of which only a small portion could be seen from the front yard. The paved path to the garden split off to a gazebo stationed next to a pond with a fountain and ducks. To the right of the house was a large, detached garage, big enough for a tractor-trailer. It was more beautiful than she could have imagined. In awe, she sat frozen in the truck. Adam turned off the ignition and sighed a soft smile.

"You like your house?" he asked, looking at her frozen gaze.

"I love it," she breathed out as she opened the door.

She jumped out and stumbled slowly around the front yard. Attention had been paid to the detail of every blade of grass. She walked up on the front porch and twirled and smiled, making her way to the side porch, following the path to the gazebo, and then doubling back to explore the garden. She ran and jumped and screamed for ten minutes while Adam leaned on the truck in the driveway, laughing and enjoying her joy all the while.

"Let's go inside!" Brenda shouted, running back towards Adam.

"No ma'am. That's your house. Can't step foot in there," Adam objected, raising his hands.

"Well, if it's my house and I say you can, you can," Brenda clarified.

"Sir don't like other dogs walking where he plays," Adam said, asserting his objection.

"What? Other dogs? Plays? This man done did all this. He ain't playing. He's just scared to be married, but I think we'll get there one day," Brenda naively expressed.

Adam laughed.

"What's funny?" Brenda asked.

"You really think y'all are a thing, don't you?" Adam asked in genuine shock. "I sometimes forget how young you are," he added.

"I mean I figure he's gonna love me until I hit like thirty five and my titties drop. So, I'm just stacking my bread for then, so I can afford to be a cougar to some young ball player and get my youth back," Brenda enlightened him.

"Damn. You said love," Adam said, shaking his head.

"Well, maybe not love quiet yet," Brenda rebutted.

"You're smart and useful. If you were ugly, you'd have a job. Since you're beautiful, you get something in exchange for your youth. You chose well. I've seen birds get clothes and jewelry," Adam told her.

"So, wait. Sir is finna pimp me?! I ain't fucking no fat old men. Not even for a house. Okay listen, I've saved most of my paychecks and everybody knows I can't drive. I'll run the truck off the road and you say my body flew out of the window," Brenda rambled nervously.

"Shut up," Adam interrupted. "You're not going to be with any other men. Period."

"Well, that's why this house is in my name. I can do and be with whoever I want when he gets tired of me. It's mine," Brenda continued to argue.

"He's not going to get tired of you until no one wants you," Adam explained. "He doesn't love you; he loves the energy you give his business and the boost you give his ego."

"I know this. But they're broke men that play the same game. Might as well be comfortable if I have to play the game," Brenda shrugged.

"You don't have to, you choose to," Adam said. "Go explore your house. I'll be waiting in the truck for you," he ended the conversation with a smile.

Brenda grabbed Adam's hand to stop him from leaving.

"Come inside with me. This is my house. I will allow in whoever I please," Brenda said seriously as she guided Adam behind her.

"All this time you've looked after me so well and helped me along. I thought you would be happy to see me get a house," Brenda said as she and Adam stood on her porch.

"I'm happy to see you get the house. Just disappointed to know you are his," Adam confessed.

"All this time, I figured you knew and just pretended not to for my dignity's sake," Brenda said as she let go of Adam's hand.

"Nope. He never told me. He must have recognized my attraction to you. Smart man. Wouldn't want me throwing salt in his game. I'm sure he figured you'd never initiate anything, assuming I knew. And I'd never have the confidence to approach you," Adam shrugged. "So here we are."

"Come in, Adam." Brenda pulled him through the door.

"You have been present at every joyful moment I can remember in this last year. I always have to measure up for him. He is my job and I've learned how to pretend to be happy with it, but I know the truth. I did love him in the best way I could. I gave him what I understood love to be. But if you're trying to say you think you love me, I think I love you too, " Brenda said as she began to unbutton her blouse.

Adam's blood filled the center of his body, and his trousers could not hide his excitement.

"This is mine, and I'll let in who I want," Brenda said as she placed Adam's hand on her moistness. Adam closed the door behind him, and they let their passions fly. Brenda peeped around corners as they ravaged one another's clothes to the floor, looking for a living room couch. She found it. Having Adam stripped down to his boxers, she pushed him down on the couch and knelt in front of him with wide-eyed anticipation of seeing him for the first time. He leaned back and lifted himself allowing Brenda to remove his boxers.

She sat back on her feet, in awe at the anomaly before her. She grabbed it and stared at the space in between her fingers where his girth would not allow them to touch. The veins of him looked like powerlines snaked around a tree after a hurricane.

"I don't know if we can do this," Brenda said with fearful desire.

"I'll be gentle. I promise," Adam said, obviously aware of his size.

"Sit back," Brenda said, pushing at his chest.

She grabbed him with both hands, neither completely encompassing the circumference of him. One hand on top of another, and there was still a third of him exposed from her grip, for the tasting. She planted several gentle kisses around the sensitive top of him. Feeling the twitch of him with every gently sucked kiss, Brenda moistly throbbed in tandem with anticipation. Adam's protruding veins began to glisten as she wet them with licks in between the kisses. She mapped him out. She felt pressure in a vein shoot past her thumb. Gripping the underbelly of his brick, she pinched the vein as she gently closed his opening inside the kiss of her lips, and cleared his line of the clear fluid glossing Brenda's lips.

"Not yet," Brenda said, feeling Adam getting too excited too quickly.

She let him go. They stood, and Brenda guided them on their exploration of the house. She went up the stairs and found what had to be the master bedroom. Growing impatient, Adam picked Brenda up and took a few quick, long strides to the bed. He laid her on her back and handcuffed her feet together with one hand, positioning himself with the other. His knees shook with the warmth of her lips giving him a stiff and slippery kiss. He gently increased the pressure and let up when Brenda reached around and pushed him back. It looked impossible for her small frame to receive Adam. He pushed harder, caressing her face for assurance he was not trying to hurt her. With a kiss, Adam forced through her rejections and snapped into the rubber band of her walls. His body twitched as she gripped him in place. Brenda's moans became yells as she squeezed his wrists, hoping for relief. He wanted more than just the tip in. His short, hard strokes intensified with every defeat. He laid his weight on her, and as Brenda yelled out in pleasure filled pain, Adam stopped.

He sat up and looked at Brenda, still gripping her breast, waiting to feel him again. A few moments passed and noticing his caution, Brenda looked up.

"It's okay. I know it will hurt a little until I get used to you. I can take it. Come on."

Adam looked in silence.

"What's wrong?" Brenda sat up, noticing the confused look on his face.

She looked down at him and then checked herself.

"You did not just tip dip and let your nut slip!" Brenda yelled at Adam.

"Hey! I can't help it if that happened. I can't control it!" Adam said through his embarrassment. They made their way back through the house collecting their outfits that had been scattered in various places from the doorway to the bedroom. Brenda playfully antagonized Adam about his performance.

"So, all this time you've been waiting for me?" Brenda asked Adam.

"Waiting to figure out how to approach you," Adam shrugged.

"I, real deal, thought you were gay. I never saw or heard of any women, and you were always with Sir. I figured he was really gay too and y'all both were using me as a cover. It would make sense why you were so nice to me," Brenda broke down to him.

"Where do you get these things?" Adam laughed.

"Well since it's all out there, tell me, did Sir not want me to do the tour because another woman was there?" Brenda questioned Adam.

"Naw. Sir's not that messy. He generally meets people by chance, never planned," Adam assured her.

"Whatever the reason, Sir did not argue about me not arguing about not doing the tour, so he wanted me to leave just as well as I wanted to go. He probably knows I knew about the house already," Brenda talked through the situation.

"So, do you love him?" Adam asked directly.

"I thought I did at first. I love the way he treats me. I love the comforts he provides. But when he looks at me, all he sees is my beauty and ambitions. I cannot show him my imperfections," Brenda said as she turned to look at Adam. "You see all of me and smile when I am a mess. You cover for me and keep me from falling. You laugh with me at shit that's actually funny. You remember when I farted at that dinner, and I had to leave the table because I couldn't stop laughing when you smelled something and looked directly over at me?" Brenda poured out and laughed.

"You fart so much in the car; how could I not know what your poot smells like?" Adam laughed back.

"What love I thought I had for him is dead. I love you," Brenda said, kissing Adam's hand.

10

CHARGE IT TO THE GAME BABY

The house was back in order, and anything knocked out of place was put back. The mandatory meeting was over, and Sir would be arriving soon. Adam sat outside in the truck so as not to be alone in the house with Brenda at Sir's arrival. They spoke on the phone as she prepared dinner with the fresh foods stocked in the fridge.

"How long do you think he'll want me to work for him?" Brenda asked.

"Forever," Adam laughed. "He'll want you around for as long as you're good at your job."

"Maybe I can play like I fell off a bike and I'm slow now. And you can ask him if you could take me in. Out of compassion , cuz that rock I hit when I fell off that bike really messed me up," Brenda offered up.

"Yep. Shut up," Adam said at the ludicrous suggestion.

"I have enough money saved up to quit. I could afford the taxes on this property. Let's just quit," Brenda alternatively suggested.

"No. You can't quit Sir. We'll talk later. He's here," Adam ended the conversation, seeing the lights of an SUV coming down the tree tunnel entrance to the property.

Refocusing his attention to his job Adam got out of the car to be at attention when Sir pulled up.

"Good evening, Adam. Thank you for this. Is she excited?" Sir asked in his usual flat voice.

"Good evening. You're welcome. And yes, Sir, she is. She ran around the yard for a solid ten minutes when we arrived," Adam reported.

"Good. And the clients had many wonderful things to say about the building. Let me go make a good day great. You can take the rest of the evening off. It's been a long day," Sir said as he patted Adam on the shoulder.

"Thank you, Sir," Adam said as he turned to get in the truck and head home for the night.

Sir walked slowly to the entrance of the house ,looking around to admire what he had built for Brenda. It was beautiful. He was confident that he had given her what she'd asked for. He opened the door to the smell of steaming potatoes and garlic. Hearing the door open, Brenda shouted to greet him, "Sir!" Her call was unanswered. She removed her apron and washed her hands before exiting the kitchen towards the front door.

"Sir!" She called out again.

"In here!" He yelled back.

Brenda walked towards the living room where he sat with his head up to the ceiling. He loosened his tie and gave Brenda a soft smile as she entered the room.

"Do you like your house?" Sir asked.

"I love it," Brenda smiled at him as she walked over to join him on the couch. "Would you like me to run you a bath or would you like to shower tonight?" Brenda dutifully inquired.

"A bath sounds nice. Today was long. I'll tell you all the nice things the clients said about your building while you scrub my back," Sir said, stretching his arm back out of his blazer.

"Forgive me. I've already eaten so you didn't have to cook tonight," Sir added.

"No worries. I'll turn the stove off and run you a bath right away," Brenda cheerfully replied.

"Thank you," Sir said as they both stood to leave the living room.

Brenda hastened to turn off the stove and cover the food before making it upstairs to the master bedroom where Sir was undressing. She turned the water on and put salts and oils at the base of the tub. As the water filled, she gathered a washcloth, soap, and towel for him. Sir sat on the edge of the bed with only his shirt removed. Brenda walked out of the bathroom and gasped at the gun that was resting on Sir's waist.

"Why are you walking around with a gun on you?" Brenda nervously asked.

"Do you really think I'd build all this and not have cameras to watch it?" Sir eerily laughed.

Brenda froze in fear.

Sir stood up and walked towards Brenda calmly.

"I told you I had too much money for a wife. I told you. I told you. None of you are ever satisfied. You always want love! What's love?! Are you hungry?! Are you dirty?! Are you broke?! Then what else do you need?" Sir yelled.

Brenda shrouded down in fear as the vibrations of his voice rippled through her chest. There was nothing for her to say in that moment.

"So, what if I have other women? They don't see you and you don't see them! And I can afford it! Can Adam afford the time I paid for?! Can he?!" Sir yelled.

"No, he can't because I pay him!" Sir continued as he drew the gun holster in his belt.

"Why?!" Sir asked, pointing the gun at Brenda's head.

"Because you were my job. You paid me for my time, but my feelings weren't included," Brenda yelled back with desperation in her voice.

"It's always the same story. You can't buy love," Sir smirked.

Taking advantage of Sir's prolonged soaking in the moment ,Brenda lunged forward, grabbing the gun with both hands attempting to wrestle it from him.

BANG! They both took a deep breath. *BANG!* Brenda's ears rang as she stumbled the three feet to the bathtub and rested her tired body on the edge. Her eyes filled with tears, blood gloving both her hands; she dropped the gun.

She had managed to pull the gun away from Sir, but in the tussle, one bullet went through her arm, another through his head. Sir's body collapsed to the floor, and the blood began to paint the brown marble floors red. Snapping out of a trance, Brenda steadied her breathing and rushed downstairs to call the police.

"Nine One One. What's the location of your emergency?" the receiver asked.

"I don't know! I don't know! Just please help! GPS me! It's a house off of Monroe! I need an ambulance, quick!"

The sirens were heard approaching from a mile up the road. The silence of the country was broken with sirens and Brenda's screams directing the EMTs to her. They rushed to the floor to Sir, who, in

71

Brenda's eyes, appeared dead. Another group of EMTs lifted Brenda up and guided her around the blood on the floor to a stretcher where they could relocate her outside for treatment.

"What happened here, ma'am?" the officer asked as antiseptics were applied to Brenda's wounds.

"I was getting his bath ready and he was yelling and I was scared and he had the gun and I shot him," Brenda, barely coherent, cried to the officer.

"Okay, okay, ma'am, calm down," the detective said.

"She sustained a gunshot wound to the arm and some blunt force trauma to the head," the EMT reported before the detective walked away to consort with his colleagues.

Brenda got a shot of morpheme for pain and was out.

She woke up in her apartment in the city to the squeal of a hot tea kettle. Sam walked over and sat in the bed beside her.

"So, you rich, rich now? Like you get shot at, rich?" Sam joked as her and Brenda's eyes connected for the first time in months.

"Shut up," Brenda laughed as she sat up to embrace her.

"So, what the hell is going on that you around here getting while bullet piercing? Don't follow the trends girl, that is not fashionable?" Sam masked her concern in her jokes.

"It's a long story," Brenda said, rubbing her head. "What time is it?" Brenda asked turning her feet to get out of bed.

"Time for you to lay yo ass back down," Sam said, rushing to turn Brenda's feet back onto the bed before she realized what was going on.

Just as Sam snatched the cover back over Brenda's legs, Brenda shouted, "What the hell is going on?! How long was I asleep?!"

"A month," Sam informed her. "Listen, the lady told me that if you wake up, just act normal so you don't have no psychological break. I ain't doing this right. Just lay down and go back to sleep. Imma call this lady, and she'll be here in a lil' bit to explain all this to you," Sam nervously ranted as she paced back and forth, looking for Brenda's medical folder with contacts.

"A month?!" Brenda said, sitting up, looking around in confusion.

"Lay back! I think they said it's not good for the baby for you to just get up and start moving!" Sam yelled in concern as she flipped through the folder she found to call the emergency contact physician.

"Baby?!" Brenda yelled. "What baby?!"

"Huh?" Sam said, realizing her mistake in telling her directly out of her coma that she is pregnant.

"You heard me, hoe! What baby?!" Brenda said sharply to Sam.

"I said getting up quick might not be good for you MAYBE! MAAAAYYYYBEEEE!" Sam stretched her lie.

Brenda plopped back on the bed, looked at the ceiling, and let out a deep sigh.

"The lady who knows what she's doing is on her way. She told me to tell you you're okay, we love you, and you're in a safe place," Sam said, walking back to Brenda's bedside having called the doctors to come.

"Do you know your name?" Sam said slowly and loudly.

"My mind is fine, Sam. Stop acting crazy," Brenda said in aggravation.

"You sure? What's two plus two? What's four plus four? What comes after nine one one?" Sam ran off her questions.

"Yes. Four. Eight. Zero zero twenty four." Brenda answered.

"Ahhhhhhhh! You're okay!" Sam screamed as she certified Brenda's health.

"Now tell me. Who's the daddy?" Sam asked.

THOU SHALL
HONOUR THE
GIRL CODE
Tanya's Story

KEAIDY BENNETT

PROLOGUE

Everyone already sees me as a menace. For as long as I've been alive, I've always heard, "It's Tanya's fault," or "Tanya took it." My all-time favorite one to hear was, "Tanya's going to end up getting killed or going to jail one day." To fight back, I eventually learned to shut the fuck up. I stopped explaining myself to motherfuckers who didn't want to understand me.

That worked… until it didn't.

Now, I'm here trying to squeeze my whole life into a short story because, in less than twenty-four hours, shit is about to get real.

Truthfully, I don't know what's going to happen. Maybe I'll succeed in getting Patrick Bennett to expose himself on camera. My goal is to finally prove that he's the spawn of Satan. No. For real. This man should be stowed away in a dungeon far…far away from all of civilization. Sure, he's charismatic and successful, but he's also a narcissistic asshole who preys on the women who blindly love him. Trust me – I know.

For those of you who have no idea what's going on here, let me give you a quick run-down.

My name is Tanya Isabella Sanchez. People who know me would recognize me as the villain in Tammy's story. If you would have read the Charge It to the Game series by Keaidy Bennett, you would know that.

Originally, I wasn't going to say anything, but I can't let this one slide. I just think it's funny how ya'll made mad assumptions of me without ever hearing my side of the story. That's crazy, but here we are.

Regardless of what you or anyone else thinks, Tamia Santiago has been my best friend since I was a child, so you would be insane to believe I would ever do anything to jeopardize the one real friendship I've ever had. Contrary to what you motherfuckers decided to believe, it was a choice for my sisters and me to only hang around each other. In fact, my mother had always taught us that we are all we have in this world, so we didn't need friends. I lived like that... until I met Tee.

Truth be told, I couldn't care less about clearing up my side of the story for the rest of you. I'm only doing this because if I've learned anything about Patrick Bennett, it's that his ass cannot and should not ever be trusted. Pretty soon, one of us will have to **Charge It to the Game**, and in this case, it looks like it's gonna be me. I just need my girl to know the truth: no matter how outrageous shit looked, I *always* honored the girl code.

1
CHARGE IT TO THE GAME BABY

"Bitch! I know you hear me calling your name," I heard my mother's distinct voice shout out from my bedroom window. Despite all of the chaos happening on the busy New York streets, when Maria Sanchez speaks, you can't ignore her.

I rushed to my window to yell down below to let her know that I wasn't ignoring her.

"I was napping, Ma," I lied in an effort to avoid having her yell back anything crazy. "What's up?"

Despite the tone of her voice a few moments ago, the excitement on my mother's face and her gestures for me to come down told me that something good was about to happen.

Without another word, I slid my chancletas on my feet, and rushed down the stairs to meet her.

"What's with all of the excitement?" I asked eagerly. "I've never seen you like this."

"Bitch," my mother started. "That damn Delino Santiago came over here asking about you and your sisters. He said he needs you guys to do a huge favor for him."

What the fuck does that have to do with me, is what I really wanted to ask, but because I had never seen my mother so giddy, I decided to play into it.

"Oh yeah," I asked trying to fake a little excitement. "What kind of favor is it?"

"Apparently, that brat child of his needs to be picked up from the airport, and he isn't going to be able to do it."

Bitch, I'm not a fucking babysitter. Can't he get one of the niggas on his payroll to do it?

"I don't know about this, Ma," I started before her demeanor completely switched.

"I'm not asking you to do this, Tanya. You and your sisters will be going to that airport to pick the bitch up, and you will be on your best behavior. Do you understand?"

Even at the tender age of sixteen, I knew just who to play crazy with, and my mother was not the one. Despite my reservations, I nodded my head to avoid having to hear anymore of her mouth.

"I don't care what you have to do to be friends with this girl, ya'll have to get along," she continued. "And you better not fuck this up like you do everything else."

How the hell do you raise me to not make friends, and now, all of a sudden, you are pushing me to befriend someone I don't even know? In that moment, I had a lot of questions that I wanted to ask her—especially when it came to Delino Santiago, but I knew better than to press her right now. It was early in the day, and that meant my mother didn't have her fix yet.

Unlike most addicts, you would never know by looking at her that she was hooked on some of the same drugs that people were out here killing themselves with.

"Where are your other sisters?" my mother asked as she pulled her cigarette holder out of the place in her bra that she always kept it tucked in.

"I dunno," I lied while she lit up one of those shitty smelling cancer sticks.

Maria Sanchez pulled a long hard toke before she exhaled and started talking trash about how she couldn't trust me to handle this. She also mentioned that she would kill me herself if this didn't go as she planned. Thanks to many years of training, I just tuned my ears off to her foolishness. I had a lot to do later that night, and I wasn't about to let her piss me off before I had a chance to handle my business.

"I know you hear me little girl," my mother snapped, interrupting my peaceful fantasies about what was to come that night.

"Sorry, Ma…. what did you say?" I asked as she brought me back to my sad reality.

"Keep playing crazy with me, bitch. You'll soon find out why they used to call me Pound Town Mary back in my day," she said before she blew the smoke directly into my face.

I always assumed it's because you took a lot of dick to have three kids by three different niggas while you added to your list to supply your habit, but maybe I'm wrong. It took every bone in my body to keep that thought to myself, but I couldn't afford to get in trouble today.

"I might not look it now, but once upon a time I could grab a bitch that tried me with lighting speed and give her a few pounds upside her head to let her know that I am not the fucking one. Don't find out today," she threatened.

My mom was only 5'1, so the extra weight she had put on after having kids really did a number on her self-esteem. Maria Sanchez was still cute in the face even with the extra love in the waist, but she always had to make it a point to talk about her excess pounds whenever she mentioned something from her past.

I watched as she attempted to flip her dry, stiff ass shoulder length hair back from her face. Her shit was so fried from years of trying to hide from the beauty of her kinky curly 4C hair, but that didn't stop her from putting a hot comb to it every chance she could.

Although my mother could fool the rest of the world, standing this close to her under the hot New York sun allowed me to see every single wrinkle and blemish that her secrets were beginning to expose. The dark circles under her eyes from nights of binging were so hard to hide that my mother had begun a full make-up routine in the mornings, but the summer's heat was literally melting her mask right off her face.

"Anyway," my mother said before she paused to enjoy another long hit. "Delino said he is going to pay for you guys doing him this favor. All he needs you to do is show the rich bitch around the city while he wraps up some meetings that he has for the day, but I need you to get in close with this hoe."

I was beginning to reach my limit with my mother and all her shit for the day. Usually, I could tune her out and tolerate her on most days, but whenever she began to get delusional with her thoughts about the neighborhood drug lord, Delino Santiago, I immediately wanted to slap some sense into her.

"Now, remember," she continued as she attempted to flip her hair again. "Your full name is Tanya Isabella Sanchez, and our family is originally from Puerto Rico," my mother coached me on the same lie she has had me reciting for as long as I could remember. "Put a little Latin flair on the way you handle yourself around her. I can't have my future baby daddy thinking I'm not good enough for him."

Bitch you aren't. The man only runs around here with Spanish women who are bad with shit going for themselves. Mr. Santiago is not checking for your miserable ass. How long are you willing to continue a lie for a man who has never said more than a couple sentences to you at a time?

"I got you, Ma, but I got to go," I spoke up, hoping to excuse myself from her illusions. "When do we have to go through with this anyway?" I asked while secretly praying that it was for any day other than today.

"He said he was going to call me later tonight with the details," my mother responded, unable to hide the smile creeping up on her face. "This might be my chance, bitch. I'm about to get my man," she declared confidently.

Don't roll your eyes, Tanya. Don't do it. We need to go through with this shit tonight. If you say or do the wrong thing, you'll be forced to babysit your mom's ass through another binge again. Tonight is about to change the game for us.

"Hopefully," I lied as I adjusted my shorts. They were already short as hell, but my thick thighs seemed to eat them right up even though I was only standing there.

Unlike my mother, I was proud of the beautiful black heritage my ancestors blessed me with. I had hips and ass for days, and since I had a big chest to match, I could easily convince anyone that I was grown enough to handle the business that was about to go down tonight.

"Don't be funny with me, puta," my mom stated in her attempt to add that *Latin flair* she was desperate to imitate.

"Si, señora," I responded back with a smirk on my face. I just wanted to appease the bitch and put this conversation behind me.

"Where are you trying to rush out to?" she asked in an attempt to continue the exhausting conversation.

At this point, I would rather be anywhere but here, I wanted to respond, although I knew better.

"You remember that boy Derrick? Well, he invited me out tonight," I declared while adjusting my shorts again.

"Bitch, you out here giving away your pussy for free?" she asked just a little too loudly for me.

I might be your child, but I'm not trying to follow in your stupid-ass footsteps. You clearly have no desire to offer us a better life, and after Derrick introduces me to Patrick Bennett tonight, I will finally be able to put you and this hellhole behind me once and for all. Again, instead of saying what I truly wanted, I just mustered up another half lie to get her off my ass.

"Of course not, Ma. You taught us better than that. *If* I allow this boy to play around with me tonight, I'll make sure he pays for it first," I stated with a half-smile.

"Thank God you aren't as dumb as you look, girl," my mom responded before choking on the smoke she had just inhaled.

Instant Karma. My favorite. Maybe the next one will finally rid my sisters and me from you once and for all. Sadly, fate had other plans for me. Maybe it was my mother's attempt to make the public believe we have a normal relationship, or maybe she just enjoys tormenting me. I had to listen to my mother spend almost two hours talking about her ideal life with Delino. Not once in her long-ass rant did she even mention where I would fit in if her wildest dream did come true.

As if my two sisters had sensed my inability to hold my tongue any longer, I saw them out of the corner of my eye as they approached us on the stoop. I turned to look at them, and for a moment, I felt this thing in my chest that I thought could have been love. My sisters smiled at me, and for a moment, I forgot about every single fight or mean word we've ever said to each other.

That moment didn't last long.

"There are my girls," my mother stated with a sweetness in her voice I had never heard used with me. "Where have my two babies been?"

She's so fucking fake. I wonder why she tries to play me like I'm the problem and then treats these two like royalty.

"Nada, Mami," Nina, my older sister spoke up first. "We just went for a walk around the block."

Out of all of us, Nina Sanchez was the tallest. Since her daddy was a white man, her story of being a Puerto Rican princess was much more believable than for Tiffany, my baby sister, and me, but my mom left us no choice. It didn't matter who we really were. It wasn't good enough for that man she was married to only in her head.

"Well, seeing you two is exactly what I needed to lift my spirits," my mother sweetly declared before reaching out to embrace them.

Although my sisters both claimed to notice the way my mother treated me like an unwanted stepchild, they seemed to enjoy receiving the love I lost hope of ever getting. Outwardly, I respected my mother, but that was only for survival. These New York streets are too dangerous and cold for me to play games with her. Instead, I'm forced to fake the funk quietly while I live with my biggest hater.

"Don't you have a date coming up soon?" Tiffany asked with a wink as she finally spoke up. "Shouldn't you be getting ready for that?"

Shouldn't you be losing all of that weight you fat miserable bitch? That was my desired response, but because I'm always outnumbered, it made no sense to speak up.

"Thanks, sis, I was having too much fun with this *family time* that I almost let it slip my mind," I lied straight through my teeth with a smile on my face. Being the black sheep in the family meant that I learned how to do this shit early on.

Once my mother started gushing about her future baby daddy calling her later that evening, I knew it was the perfect time for me to make my exit.

As I ran up the stairs to our dingy-ass two-bedroom apartment, I couldn't help but fantasize about what would happen in just a few hours.

Growing up, I had always had a crush on Derrick Williams, but once puberty kicked in, and the man started making real money in these streets, every bitch from here to Jersey was in his face.

Sure, I could have pressed my luck to get beside him. Shit, my body and my face looked better than most women twice my age, but I have bigger goals than the neighborhood dope boy. I needed to catch a larger fish if I was ever going to get myself out of my fucking nightmare.

I took a quick shower, and then decided to throw on some jeans and the only polo shirt I owned. Even though I was wearing more clothes than I usually would, I was confident that my face card was enough.

I took one glance in the mirror and was immediately reminded of why these bitches I live with probably can't stand me. Even though I was short as hell, just like my mama, my Coke bottle shape and my blemish-free mocha skin didn't need anything to enhance how naturally beautiful I was.

Satisfied with the image in front of me, I put on my best pair of sneakers. Don't ask me for the name because I can't remember now. They were just some all-black sneakers that I never got bullied for wearing.

"Derrick is here," I heard Nina shout from the stoop below. "Bring your ass on, girl."

How about you worry about your damn self? I knew my sisters well enough to know that if this meeting went how I hoped, they would be coming around acting just as fake as their mama. I mean their *mami*. I would hate to fuck around and get out of character.

I grabbed my knock-off Louis Vuitton purse and rushed downstairs.

"Listen boy," my mama said with pure agitation in her voice. "Don't you dare make a pass at Tanya or you're going to have to deal with me. I know all about your kind."

Lady, shut up. The only thing you know how to do is hate on yourself and the one child that looks and acts the most like you.

"Te amo, Mami," I said before leaning in to kiss my mother on the cheek since the only time I would be able to receive any kind of affection from her had to take place in the comfort of strangers.

"Um-hm," she slid in while never removing her hard gaze from Derrick.

"Thank you, Ms. Sanchez. I really appreciate you for allowing me to take Tanya out tonight," Derrick responded sweetly before he flashed that hypnotizing smile of his.

For a moment, I wasn't sure if his statement was genuine or not. Even though I have and always will be confident in my sex appeal, Derrick was a senior at our high school, and because of who he was becoming, he could literally have any girl that he wanted.

Tanya....are those feelings that we are feeling right now? Turn them off immediately. And just like that, the warm fuzzy feelings that were brewing in the pit of my stomach disintegrated into nothing.

My mom didn't respond and the corny faces my sisters were making were awkward as hell.

"See ya'll later," I said with my first real smile of the night. I grabbed Derrick's hand and led him down the stoop. Then, without waiting for him to give any direction or instruction, I turned right. We walked a few blocks down before Derrick finally spoke up.

"I only let you get away with that shit because I didn't want any more weird energy from ya moms, but if the bitch ever talks to me like that again she'll leave me no choice. Got it?"

Even though I heard him. I decided not to respond. I was already on edge with everything that had transpired throughout my exchange with my mom, and I was just ready to get to the money.

"Yo," Derrick said as he stopped walking. "I realize that you've known me since I was a kid, so you think I'm just talking, but I'm not."

"Yes, sir," I responded with a half-smile.

"Anyway, you know I've started to make a name for myself, so now I got a reputation to protect..." was all I managed to hear. Despite us taking a train and a bus to get to our destination, my mind was completely absent from my body and that moment with him.

I wanted to listen to his story, but something in the atmosphere wouldn't allow me the chance to. Instead, I completely zoned out.

I haven't written a poem in forever. Why? Right now, the wind is singing, the lights are dancing through the sunset, and everything is a story all by itself. Why haven't we picked up our notebook in months?

Am I afraid of the revelations of just how dark the pit of my soul is

Or am I running from the fact that parts of my stories still have holes

Since I won't always be honest — even to myself.

It hurts to be rejected from the one person you yearn for more than most

To be banished from your creator's womb only to be shunned for your unique genetic makeup — one that resembles a reflection that hurts her too much to see

Is that why she refuses to see me — for me?

Do I remind her of every poor choice she took to arrive to this moment in time?

Or does this illusion she has of me being her competition have her too blind to see

I'm just a little black girl lost in the sauce

In a sea of everything I think I can be

And every reason why I'll never be able to achieve it.

With no lifeline on which road is less scary to take.

And no hope for better days

I force myself to make them up

Because the truth is — I've waited long enough.

As much as it pains me to come to the revelation that I've regrettably come to

It seems as though no one is coming to rescue Tanya — if that is even my real name.

No one is coming to rescue me.

As the great Calvin Ockletree once said,

"Is this how a child of God is supposed to feel?"

Because for real — how is this real?

In all relationships it seems like I'm promised things that I'll never receive.

From my mother

To my savior
To my raggedy daddy who is too busy building new homes while collecting
albums of family portraits like trophies
Tanya never seems to fit into the picture.
She's always too much
Or not enough
But how does everyone know someone who is a foreigner even to me?
As I stand in front of the mirror finally able to see me
I take a moment to adjust my view.
No longer looking through the outlines that were present from the perception of
others — I finally see a new person.
I know why I couldn't write a single word before arriving to this desolate place
A space in my mind that I thought I could abandon forever.
Down the hallways of time
Past the empty corridors of rejection and shame
In a dark room surrounded by dreams that would never come to pass
Lived a little girl whose only desire was to be acknowledged.
The little girl with the Mickey Mouse plush toy in her hands and the spark of
faith in her eyes
Is me at about three or four.
Is it normal to have memories that far back?
Or have I grown too comfy with allowing my mind to talk to me in the same
tone of a woman I wish I could forget?
Anyway, the frail child had grown malnourished from surviving on mere
crumbs of love from those who she had to trust to survive.
One who only hoped that she would someday be worthy enough to be
remembered so she could eventually leave this place.
For the first time ever, I looked at her — not with disgust like I had before.
No, this time I actually held space for her desperation.
"How frightening it must feel to be so small and mighty, with no one to tell
her about the magic brewing under that brown skin," I thought as I allowed
myself to step into the room that was a safe haven for her and a land of dry bones
for me.
As I thoroughly inspected her room, I finally felt compassion for myself.
"How sad it must feel to have once been so filled with endless possibilities. Is
her love for magical things the reason why I now refuse to believe in anything but
myself?"
I knelt down beside her.
Oh, how beautiful she was.

She smiled a smile that was a mile wide and reached her hand out.
Unlike the woman I was today, her pride didn't hold her back from asking
for the thing she needed most.
Did I want to be touched?
Absolutely not.
After years of trying to stay out of the way, I had learned to not ask for
something I knew was never going to come, but for a moment I realized that
maybe this is what we both needed.
We interlocked fingers and that smile of hers somehow managed to grow even
bigger.
In that moment, we both saw each other.
The good
The bad
And everything else in between – we held room for the other to have a taste of
what we needed most
For her, she just wanted the love of an adult so she could know she was not in
this cold world alone
For me, I needed a reminder that my soul wasn't as dark as I was conditioned
to believe.
In that moment, I finally knew why I had been running from poetry and
writing in that damn notebook
Sitting there with her, trying to keep it all together so her world didn't have to
crumble apart like mine had, I realized the importance of facing a part of me that
I once hated.
"I'll protect you sweet Tanya," I said with a sincere smile.
Unlike the other people I had tried to love or get close to, she didn't project her
fears. Instead, she leaned in closer and embraced me in a way I had never been
embraced.
It seems my soul was never dark, but I didn't notice that until her love showed
me a brand-new view.

"Tanya are you listening to me?" Derrick asked as he lightly grabbed my arm.

"Yes," I lied. "But can you just run that last part by me again? I want to make sure I truly understood you."

"Patrick Bennett is not an easy person to do business with. Don't come in here trying to bullshit him. If he thinks you're on trash, he'll kick you out of here—or worse. Are you sure you really want to go through with this?" Derrick asked me while searching my eyes for the truth.

"I've never been more sure of anything in my life."

2
HUNG OVER

"Bitch, you better be ready," my mother's voice roared through our tiny apartment. "You will not make a bad impression with my new daughter."

I glanced over to the clock on my nightstand. *Why the hell is she waking me up at five in the morning. I know she heard me come in just a couple of hours ago.*

I wanted to throw the blanket over my face and hide for the rest of the day, but I could hear the fire roaring deep down in her throat, and I wasn't in the mood to start my day with her crap.

I went to sit up, and I was immediately reminded of how many drinks I had the night before.

Tequila never leaves me feeling like this, I thought. *Why does it feel like the room is spinning? Why do I want to throw up right now?*

"Tanya," my mother barked out at the same time my body signaled that it was time to let go of my sins from the night before.

"Coming, Ma," I managed to muster before everything made its way up my esophagus and into the trashcan right next to my bed.

"You let that nigga get you drunk, huh?" Nina asked as she sat up. "Did you at least handle your fucking business?"

I know this bitch isn't questioning me. Unlike her, I don't have the love of a mother to fall back on.

I wanted to go off on her ass just for getting on my nerves so early in the morning, but with the way my stomach was feeling, I knew it was best to keep my fucking mouth shut.

"In case you can't tell, I'm not in the mood for any interrogations,"

I responded flatly hoping she would leave the conversation alone. I couldn't afford to have my mom and my sister on my back in this condition.

"You're hungover, asshole," Nina responded as she reached under her bed to her stash of snacks. I heard her ruffle through the beat-up shoe box before she pulled out a can of ginger-ale. "Drink this, and I'll go see what the fuck she needs."

Without waiting for my response, I watched as my sister served me that hot off-brand soda and handled something that was silently filling me with anxiety.

Damn. I wonder why she's being so nice to me. No one ever offers to help me with anything unless it immediately benefits them.

Despite my confusion in that moment, I was relieved. Even though my stomach wouldn't show it, I was still living on the high from the night before.

***

"Don't come in with that boss bitch energy," Derrick continued as we made our way to the sports bar where we were meeting Patrick. "Oh, and I told him you were eighteen, so make sure you act like it and continue the story if he asks you."

Derrick opened the door for me, and for the first time that evening, my nerves felt like they could overtake me.

"You got this Tanya," Derrick said barely above a whisper as if he could feel my vibe. "Do you need me to get you something to drink?"

You shouldn't drink Tanya. You don't want Patrick to think you have any vices that would make you unreasonable to work with.

"Uh," I started as I struggled to find a confident answer.

"You need one," he responded with a chuckle. "We're going to walk over to the bar, and we are going to have a drink. When they call us over to speak with him, I need you to do something other than act awkward."

They walked over to the bar in the center of the room.

This is what adults be making a fuss about. There is nothing special about being in this shit.

"What can I get you two?" The bartender asked as he wiped down the bar.

"A rum and coke for the lady, and I'll have my usual, please,"

Derrick stated as he pulled out my seat.

His usual? Boy you are barely legal. Do these people know that you are still in high school?

The bartender gave me a quick glance over. While I've always been placed with the body of a grown woman, my baby face would always give it away.

"She's good," Derrick stated as if he could read what the bartender was thinking. "We're business associates with La Familia."

La Familia? Who the hell is that? I thought we were here to see Patrick. Suddenly, there were a million questions that I wanted to ask Derrick, but I knew that now was not a good time.

"In case you wanted to know," Derrick stated as he leaned in closely to me, "La Familia is the organization that controls these streets. Haven't you ever wondered why Delino and Patrick can both do what they do and it not cause a war? Well, it's because a few very elite men are the ones who get to control the players on the board.

"Delino is a part of those elite men, but he'll never admit it. Personally, I think he allows Patrick to move the way he does because if shit ever got hot for him, I'm sure he plans to let Patrick take the fall." Derrick paused for a moment as the bartender returned with our drinks. Once he was out of earshot, Derrick continued.

"I'm confident that Patrick knows this, but he's such a grimy ass nigga, he needs the protection of La Familia. That motherfucker has been robbing, killing, and pimpin' for decades. Do you know how many people would kill that bastard if they knew they could?"

I knew I shouldn't, but I couldn't help but glance over at Patrick Bennett. His stature made him impossible to miss, even in a crowded room like this. But when you add his charm and charisma to the mix, you could almost catch a nut just from being around his magnetic, masculine energy.

"Don't let his charm fool you," Derrick began again as if he had read my thoughts, too. "He's a shark, and he isn't somebody you should ever put your trust into."

I grabbed my drink and took a big swig. Derrick wasn't the first person to tell me such dark things about Patrick, and while I was a little intimidated, I was also intrigued.

***

"She's just in one of her moods," Nina said as she walked back into the room to climb into her bed.

"Well, what did she say?" I asked as my stomach finally seemed to settle a little from the ginger-ale I had been sipping on.

"Tomorrow we'll be picking up the rich bitch from the airport. Your mom has a mile long list of everything she wants us to get to prepare for it. Anyway," Nina said as she attempted to shrug off what our mother said. "What happened with Patrick?"

"Oh nothing," I lied as I attempted to lay down and get comfortable again. "You know what they say about that miserable ass nigga."

For the first time ever, I wanted to tell my sister the truth. I wanted to tell her that it went better than I could have ever dreamed of, but Patrick was firm. No one was to ever know that we were working together, so I wasn't allowed to tell a soul.

"So, you basically went out and just got drunk last night?" Tiffany spoke up.

"I guess if that's how you want to look at it," I responded while trying to mask the irritation in my voice. "I don't always complain, but I be going through shit too. It was nice to forget about some shit for a while."

"Tanya, I know you better than this," Nina spoke up. "Are you sure you're telling us the truth?"

"Bitch, I'm not perfect," I stated, not bothering to mask my irritation. "I didn't accomplish the dreams that I had set out for myself, so I had a few drinks to take the edge off. Can we just talk about something else?"

Both sisters decided not to press the issue any further. I sighed a sigh of relief as I turned over in my bed to reminisce on my life-changing meeting the night before.

***

"Can you take this drink to the table over there?" the bartender asked me as he nodded his head in the direction of Patrick's table.

Bitch I don't work here. Do it yourself, is what felt like a more natural response to me; however, I had apparently been summoned.

"Go," Derrick whispered.

"But I thought…" was all I managed to get out.

"You trying to go over there or not?" the bartender asked me as he put the drink down.

Derrick's face let me know that there had been an obvious change of plans.

Despite my reservations, I picked the drink up and made my way to his table.

Play it cool, Tanya. You got this.

"Here you are, sir," I stated as I put the drink down in front of him.

Patrick looked down at the drink and then he looked back up at me.

"Have a seat," he demanded. The lack of emotions in his voice and on his face made it incredibly difficult to read him. For years, I could read the vibe in the room. It's my favorite survival tactic. While it was a little nerve-racking , it was kind of nice to be outside of my usual comfort zone.

"The drink is for you," he said as he slid it in front of me. As if that were some sort of sign, everyone within earshot of the table suddenly moved to another section of the bar.

"Thank you," I responded timidly. Without the comfort of my bad bitch attitude, I wasn't quite sure how to handle myself with him.

"So why are you here?" he asked with his eyes piercing a hole through my soul.

I need a job, but if you keep staring at me with those brown eyes, I might be here for more than business.

For the first time ever, I decided to use the example of that little girl in my poem. I decided to be vulnerable and tell him what I needed.

"I really need help," I said as I adjusted myself in my seat. "My living situation is toxic as hell, and there is no way I can afford to live on my own out here."

Emotionless, Patrick responded, "So why not get a fucking job?"

"I can't," I responded too quickly. *Damn. He's not allowed to know that we are still in high school and unable to get a decent paying job in the city.* "I guess what I'm really trying to say is that I can't clock in for someone and slave my time for a job that won't provide me with the life I deserve," I responded, hoping it wasn't obvious that I had told him something that was only half true.

"I realize that you don't know me, but people are saying that you have the power to change people's lives, and I just really need that kind of energy around me. I can't depend on the housing situation with my mother, and if I don't find another solution fast, I'm afraid of what I'll be forced to do out of desperation." That was an absolute fucking fact.

I needed something, and I needed it now.

"While your story is unfortunate, why the fuck do you think I would be interested in helping?" Patrick asked. By his demeanor, it was hard to read if he was being an asshole or if he just genuinely talked that way.

"I have a lot of skills that I think would be useful to you," I started, not even bothering to hide my anxiousness. "I can be an ear to the streets. I can cook, clean, suck dick, and anything else you may need or want help with."

For the first time since I walked over to his table, Patrick let out a chuckle.

"You know I have plenty of women offering similar services," he responded once his laughter subsided. "Most of them are rich and don't come with their hand out. Again, why should I be interested in helping you?"

"I know that you and Delino are working some of these same blocks. I'll be working closely with his only daughter soon. I could be your ear inside of his entire organization." While I never had any plans of getting close to the bitch, Patrick wasn't buying anything I had to say. That's why I knew I had to do something big.

"I'm not sold," Patrick stated as he signaled for the bartender to bring him something. "But I'll give you the chance to convince me. The bartender is going to bring over another drink for you. On the napkin will be an address. Do you think you're capable of meeting me without telling a soul?"

"Of course," I responded. "I won't tell anyone."

"So, what are you going to explain to your boy over there?" Patrick asked since he knew I came there with Derrick.

"Oh, don't worry about that. I'm only this shy and vulnerable with you. No one else knows this version of me exists," I responded back confidently.

Again, he chuckled. *Sir, keep laughing. I'm trying to giggle you out of those drawers and see if what they say about Jamaican men is true.*

"Listen, Tanya, I'm sure you've heard scary stories about me. You'd be smart to believe them," he stated with a sly smile still perched on his face. "This is your chance to walk away and act like this conversation never happened. If you meet me at that address, you better be ready to protect my fucking business."

The tone of his voice brought goosebumps to my skin, and for some reason instead of being afraid of the 6'6 giant who had basically just threatened me to make a smart choice, my panties got moist.

"Yes, sir," I responded.

3
GAME TIME

"Welcome home, Tee," my sisters and I said in unison. Our mother made us practice that all morning. She was adamant that we were not allowed to fuck this up for her.

"Where is my father?" The rich bitch responded coldly. "Also, Tee is a name reserved for close family and friends. Ya'll can call me Tammy," she continued.

I have some other things that I would prefer to call you, but I can't let you bring me out of character this early, is what I really wanted to say to her. Instead, I put on my best face and decided to give her the same fake energy that I give my mother.

"He's at home waiting for you. I'm Tanya," I declared with the fakest smile I've ever given. "These are my sisters. That's my older sister Nina, and that's our baby sister Tiffany." I pointed at each one to help her put names and faces together. "Your dad asked us to come get you to hopefully give you some time to get used to being in the big city."

"That's great," Tammy huffed. "He hasn't seen me almost all my life, and he didn't even have the decency to pick me up on his own. I'm sure this is going to be an interesting trip."

For the first time since we spoke, a part of me could feel her disappointment. *Maybe she's not miserable. Maybe, just like me, she puts on a tough exterior so she doesn't have to hide that little girl inside of her that is scared.*

"Shit," Tiffany said as she finally spoke up. "I wish my daddy was yo' daddy. I wouldn't complain if I was you."

"That's easy to say," Tammy responded without looking in her direction. "He isn't your dad, so you don't know what kind of father he actually is. Can we please just hurry up and get out of here? I've had a long day, and I just want to get where I gotta go."

Oh yeah. She's definitely too scared to say what she's really feeling.

We gave into her request to not talk, and we just helped her with her items so we could make our way back to the neighborhood.

It was kind of interesting watching someone who had never been to New York. Despite her tough demeanor, she seemed to have the excitement as a child as she eagerly looked at everything that was fighting for her attention.

In an effort to impress her future daughter, my mother had allowed Nina the chance to drive her car. Apparently, Tammy was too good to experience public transportation, at least that's how my mom made it seem.

"Your dad owns a few spots out here, but for some reason, he chooses to live over here in Bedford-Stuyvesant," Nina stated as she put the car in park. "Nobody calls it that out here, though. We all just call it Bed-Stuy.

Your dad lives in this building on the third floor. Go put your shit up, and we'll show you around."

I spoke up to offer to help the girl with her things, but she immediately shot me down. Fortunately for her, I was good friends with rejection, so her attempt to introduce us didn't work out the way she had hoped.

"Your pops says you're from Florida," I started as we made our way to her stoop.

"You have no idea," she responded while staring at all of the chaos around her.

"Brooklyn isn't as bad as it looks or appears on the movies and T.V. It just takes some getting used to, is all," I continued. "Watch your stuff, don't stare at nobody. Oh, and if shit pops off, you didn't see or hear nothing."

Before we could make it up the stairs, I heard Derrick's voice behind us.

"Ayo shorty," he yelled out. "Come here, let me talk to you."

I didn't need to turn around to see who it was, but I was curious to know if he was alone or not. I hadn't heard from Patrick since that one night we had together, and I wanted to know what was up with him.

"Damn," I whispered to Tammy. "That's Derrick. He's fine, has money, and I heard his pipe game was crazy. You need to go talk to that one." Now, I'm sure if my sisters heard me, they would think that it was weird that I was hyping this girl to go talk to my crush. At that moment, I didn't care about that. I needed to get close to someone who had access to Patrick.

To my surprise, she didn't take my advice. Instead, she continued walking up the stairs as if she hadn't heard a word I just said. Tammy had managed to slide into the building while someone was coming out, so I used that time to get next to one of the boys with Derrick.

"Hey handsome," I said seductively, hoping that he would buy into my bullshit. "How are you doing today?"

"Bitch, what do you want?" the boy responded with a laugh. "You're never this nice, so I know you're on trash."

Even though I had no idea who the boy was, I thought his response was hilarious. Once he started laughing, I knew I had him right where I wanted him.

We continued the conversation because I needed to get him comfortable enough to start opening up to me. I watched from the corner of my eyes until I saw the rich bitch come out of the building and join my sisters.

This nigga probably doesn't know shit about Patrick. Matter of fact, how do I press myself close enough to his circle without being obvious?

Then, it suddenly hit me. The bartender had to know how to get in contact with Patrick. *Instead of following this bitch around the city, I'll just go straight to the lion's den myself.*

I knew what I was about to do was a little risky, but I told the man I was desperate. Shit, I worked hard that night, and I needed to know something, and I needed an answer now.

I used the last couple dollars I had in my pocket to get me back to the bar. To my delight, both the bartender and Patrick were in the building.

Not sure how to proceed, I decided to walk up to the bartender and order the same drink that Derrick got me a couple nights ago.

"I'll take a rum and coke" I said as I took my seat at the bar. Once I was seated, I took a quick glance in Patrick's direction. Like the other night, he was seated at the corner booth with a few of his friends, two of which I remembered from our night together.

Unlike the other night, the bartender's service wasn't as quick or as friendly as before. After waiting for a few minutes and noticing that he had not made my drink, I attempted to get his attention again.

"Excuse me," I started before one of Patrick's boys interrupted me.

"This seat is for paying customers. Get your ass out of here," he demanded.

"This is a public place," I started. "I just want to get a drink." Despite my annoyance, I kept the tone of my voice low and leveled. I didn't want to piss Patrick off before having a chance to ask him about my money. "Can you please help me with that?" I asked as I tried to add a little sexiness to my voice. Certainly, the 6'4 dark chocolate man had to remember me from the other night.

Despite his hard exterior, he shot a quick glance at Patrick. As much as I wanted to do the same, I knew better.

"Don't do this shit again," he said barely under a whisper. "Patrick doesn't like bitches just popping up on him. Got it?"

"Yes, sir," I responded, meaning every single word.

"Yo, get the girl a drink to go," the burly man shouted to the bartender.

To go? I haven't spoken to Patrick yet. I wanted to walk straight over to his booth and demand that he speak to me, but I knew that wouldn't help me at all.

"Papi, does it really have to be a to-go drink?" I asked him once I felt calm enough to open my mouth. "You have to know why I'm here."

"I do," he responded emotionless. "If I allow you to show up whenever you want to, you'll make this a habit."

Calm down Tanya, I kept telling myself, but the emotions I was feeling were beginning to overtake me. *I need to speak to Patrick;* I wanted to shout, even though every cell in my body was terrified at what his response would be if I did.

"Please," I pleaded as I put all of my pride to the side. "I just have a couple of questions."

"All of you bitches do, but we don't move like that over here." Just as he finished his sentence, the bartender put my Styrofoam cup down with my drink inside.

"That will be ten dollars," he stated as he stood there waiting for his money.

Oh shit, I can't pay for that. Why didn't I think this through?

I pretended to feel around my pockets as if I were looking for my money, but certainly, they had to know that I would have never done the things I did the other night if I had money to buy ten-dollar drinks.

"I don't have it," I whispered.

"So, then why the fuck are you here?" the burly black man shouted. For the first time since walking into the bar, I felt ashamed as I felt the eyes of the other patrons staring in our direction.

"I just figured…" I started before I was interrupted.

"I got it," Patrick's voice roared from behind me. He gently laid his hand on my shoulder as he stretched his other hand out to give the bartender a crisp twenty-dollar bill.

Suddenly, I didn't want that drink as every hair on my body stood at full attention. I wasn't sure if I was scared or turned on. Either way, I had managed to get the man's attention as planned.

"Thank you," I said softly as I looked up at him.

"Don't thank me," Patrick responded, not bothering to make eye contact. "You're going to pay for it later."

Oh, he's definitely turning me on, I thought as I had a brief flashback about our encounter a couple of nights ago.

Patrick gave the burly man a nod, and without a word, he left Patrick and I at the bar together.

"What are you doing here?" he asked emotionless. "I thought I made myself very clear the other night."

"You did," I said barely above a whisper. "But I got worried when I put in work, and you never said anything about payment."

"Damn girl, you don't think I'm good for it?" Patrick asked playfully as he put his hands over his heart.

I laughed at his first attempt to show anything other than how rigid he could be.

"This is all new for me," I responded once my laughter stopped. "I've never done anything like I did the other night, so I just figured I would ask more questions instead of assuming the worst." That part was honest and true.

Patrick looked me up and down. Then, to my surprise, he smiled. "I always take care of my girls, ok?" he asked in a softer tone than I had heard him use before. "What do you need?"

"I guess whatever I earned from the other night," I responded. Because I'm new to this whole thing, I wasn't really sure what I earned or how much to ask for."

"That's not really how this works, baby girl," he stated as he looked around the bar. "I guess I just assumed by how forward you had been that you were familiar with this line of work. Meet me at that address tonight at 11. Make sure you wear something sexy." He said seductively before walking away.

***

I was on cloud nine. Sure, I wasn't sure about how I was going to sneak away later that evening, but I was going to see Patrick Bennett tonight. This time, he even asked me to wear something sexy.

I was halfway up the stoop to my apartment before I was violently brought back to reality.

"The rich bitch knows Estrella," Nina said worriedly as she rushed up the stairs next to me.

"What? How and what do you mean?" I asked as I immediately stopped to face her.

"I don't know what all they talked about," Nina continued. "All I know is that she started talking to the bitch in Spanish. How the fuck are we going to keep up Mami's secret if she's cool with someone who will be able to expose the truth?"

Suddenly, it felt like all of the air had been sucked out of my lungs. My mother had given us clear instructions not to fuck this up. If the rich bitch had a chance to talk to the one woman our mother told us to avoid, that means my sisters also took their eyes off the girl.

Sure, maybe my mother was delusional as hell for thinking she would ever have a shot with Delino Santiago. Either way, if she found out that we messed up her only shot of impressing the one man she wanted, I would never be able to have a real shot of having a relationship with that woman.

It took everything in me to remain calm, but I knew if I freaked out, then everything was definitely going to shit.

Instead of freaking out, I took a deep breath and attempted to answer my sister with the same emotionless tone that Patrick seemed so comfortable using.

"It's ok. We have a lot of time to figure this out. We'll just…" Obviously not impressed with my answer, my sister cut me off.

"This is not ok, Tanya. Maybe you're used to Mami being a bitch to you, but she's never acted that way with me before. I don't want to imagine what that even feels like."

Finally, someone other than me admits to noticing the difference in treatment. Patrick said something the other night. He said that sometimes you can use people's fears to control them. Maybe I'll try that out with Nina.

"Listen, sis. I get it, and that's why I don't want that for you either. I would never want to see her be this nasty with ya'll," I lied. "I've got an idea, but I'm going to need you to give me an alibi for tonight."

"Why?" Nina asked.

"You don't want Mami to know, right? Well, I think I know someone who can help us, but I need to leave here around ten and I don't want anyone asking questions. Let me see what I can do to keep this under control."

Please just take the fucking bait, I silently prayed to myself as my sister began looking around the block.

"I don't know…. but I'm desperate. What should I say if anyone asks where you are?" Nina asked.

"Tell them I was doing something to try to get in better with the rich bitch," I responded. "It's technically not a lie."

"Are you sure?" my sister asked again, not completely sold on my offer.

"I'm positive," I responded as confidently as I could. "I got us."

***

Nina went above and beyond as an alibi. Because she hates lying to Mami, she just played along as I gave some lie to get them all out of the house. The moment I said, "Delino is going to be," my mother ran to her room to get ready and out of the house. To give her a reason to get close to him, she decided to take her two favorite daughters with her. That meant I was free to do what I needed without anyone questioning me.

It was 10:35 p.m. when I left my house. To make it easier to sneak back in, I put on a track suit and just decided to wear my mother's sexiest olive-green lingerie set underneath.

Fortunately for me, the address I had been given was just a few blocks away from my house.

Just as I had done a few nights ago, I made sure that no one was following me as I turned down the block to the apartment building on the napkin. Once I got there, the young man who worked for Patrick greeted me.

"What's up beautiful?" he asked as he looked me up and down. "You working again tonight?"

"Yes," I responded flatly. While I knew I still needed to make a good impression, I immediately remembered the sour smell that came from underneath his balls when I gave him head a few nights ago.

I knew working for Patrick wasn't going to be easy, but I didn't know I was going to be subjected to dirty dicks in the process.

"Good," the young boy said as he stood up and rubbed his two hands together. "So far you've been my favorite girl to come through."

I don't know why his words bothered me. *Favorite?* What kind of work am I doing exactly?

Truthfully, I didn't know how to respond, so I decided to keep my mouth shut. The young man took that as his sign to continue.

"I want to go first tonight," he stated boldly.

First? What the hell is going on? My desperation had to have kicked in because I managed to stay completely calm.

"I'm not trying to be rude, but can you take me where I'm supposed to go, please?" I asked while trying to remain neutral.

"I want you to call me King when I hit it from the back," he responded as if he didn't hear my request. "Make sure you don't forget."

Something about the way he made his demands brought chills to my spine.

What am I supposed to say next? I thought the last time was a one-time thing.

I wanted to scream. I wanted to flame his ass with my best jokes, but I knew at that moment that my next move could be a life-changing decision. Niggas don't always know how to handle rejection. Turning to leave wasn't smart or safe. I didn't have any other options.

"Sir, I'm not sure what my job is," I responded honestly. "I don't think we are on the same page."

"Bitch, you on whatever page I say you on. Got it?" His eyes told me not to play around.

"Yes, sir," I responded flatly. As much as I wanted to throw up, I kept my composure and tried to force myself to think about something else.

Skies.

Lakes.
Oceans.
Poetry.
Fire.
Hell.
Rampage
Rosaries
When I let my brain go free on autopilot, it seems to take me to distant lands.
I used to find pleasure in those trips
As they would help me to dismiss
Hearing someone else project their shit at my tender frame.
"Fast"
Bitch what does that even mean?
I never had someone teach me the pace
Of this race
This game of life that we are playing comes with no rules
And for me – no guidance.
No one to hold my hand and say, "Baby, it's gonna be ok."
No one to say, "Baby, I love you anyway."
No.
I have to earn everything,
And even with all of my efforts, hours, and tears spent,
I still have nothing.

"Bitch bring yo' ass on then," he demanded as he took another step towards me.

Wait. Why isn't my brain still on autopilot? Why do I feel like I can't escape feeling this moment?

"Do you have anything to drink?" I asked, hoping for at least a shot of some liquid courage at this point.

"I'll let you snort some coke off of this dick," he fired back with a slight laugh.

No. Tanya. We can't.

But we need something.

Mami seems to have a decent hold on it. If she can do it, then I know I can hide it better than her.

I couldn't respond. Despite knowing the consequences, my ass wrestled with the idea of doing drugs so that I could sleep with a man to secure housing for myself.

Why are we going to a different address than the one I was originally given?
Did Patrick tell him to do this?
What if he isn't a part of Patrick's team anymore?
What if this is some sort of revenge plot for him?
Was I in the wrong place at the wrong time?
What's going to happen to me?
Will anyone know that I'm gone?
Will anyone go looking for me?
Will I ever see my mom again?
Is this really how our fucked up relationship ends?

I wanted to ask him all of the thoughts running through my brain, but I had to stay cool.

We only walked five blocks, but with each step, I was forced to push my intuition to the side, so I was exhausted. We turned left, and I continued closely behind him as he approached a large all-black SUV.

Before we could make it to the car, both of the front doors swung open.

Two men in all black stepped out and went to the back of the car. I went to the man closest to the curb, who opened the door for me. I immediately sighed a sigh of relief when I saw Patrick.

Thank God.

Like always, Patrick looked fine as hell. Even though he wasn't wearing anything flashy, his physique popping out of his tank top was a perfect view by itself.

"Ya'll niggas give us a minute," Patrick stated before the men casually moved away from the car.

"Are you always this trusting with niggas?" Patrick asked.

I couldn't read him. I wasn't sure if he was impressed or embarrassed.

"I didn't know what else to do." I answered honestly. "Some guys don't handle rejection very well."

"Where the fuck is your dad?" he asked me as he stared deeply into my eyes.

"I don't know, and I don't care," I fired back, unable to hold back my disgust.

"You really out here by yourself?" Patrick asked as he seemed to soften his tone.

"Yeah." Something about admitting it to someone else made the truth hurt more than it usually did.

"Something tells me that I shouldn't fuck with you Tanya, but I don't want to leave you like this. I hate that niggas really got women like you walking around here uncovered and shit. No protection. No guidance. No direction. What the fuck is wrong with these niggas?"

His passion for something that I agreed with immediately made my pussy wet.

I don't know, but you can be my daddy tonight, is what I wanted to say back, but I decided to play it cool.

The first time we kicked it, he made me feel so comfortable with him that I managed to tell him my family's darkest secret.

To my pleasant surprise, he just laughed it off.

"Baby girl, if that is your biggest problem, then you're blessed. Between your brains and your beauty, I'm sure you're going to figure it out." Patrick told me after we took another shot of room temperature tequila. Judging from the opened bottle in his hand, it was going to be that kind of kick back tonight.

Am I finally gonna fuck him? I know he said he was curious about my skills. I was confused when he was cool with me showing his homeboys, but he specifically asked for me to wear something sexy. He has to want me, right?

"Tanya, I know that after everything you've shared with me, it might be hard for you to believe me, but I want to make sure you're good. Not just with a place to stay, but I want you to find a good man and really take care of yourself. You deserve to finally have some peace in your life," Patrick stated.

I wanted to reach over and hug him. I wanted to pull him in and let go of all of the tears that I was feeling, but I was afraid at how he would respond. Instead, all the energy festering inside me grew to a point where I couldn't hold my words in.

"I really want to believe you, but the two people who have a financial, moral, ethical, and spiritual obligation to care for me checked out a long time ago. Why the fuck would you or anyone else stick around? You expect me to believe that *Patrick Bennett,* of all fucking people, gives a fuck about some semi-orphaned bastard? Let's be for real."

I was shocked with myself, but the freedom of spitting those words out in that moment felt therapeutic.

"You have to start thinking better of yourself, baby girl. Look at how you stressed my name," he said before he started laughing. "Why do you have to put so much of an emphasis on it? I'm just a regular nigga out here trying to make it. Don't ever put me above you like that. You deserve the best things life has to offer."

That was the first time anyone ever told me something like that. Before that moment, I had survived on the love that other people gave me. For the first time ever, I contemplated the idea that maybe I was deserving of more.

"Do you really believe that?" I asked hopefully.

"Of course," he responded as he took the bottle and poured two shots. He smiled at me as he handed one to me.

"To Tanya having the life of her dreams. May she never forget this moment—the day that she chose to fully change her life," Patrick stated.

I raised my shot glass to his as a smile crept up on my face. "Are you always this cute?"

"Hell no." He responded boldly. "I am what I am, and don't you ever forget it."

Boy, please. The way that you're sitting in this car, taking shots, and encouraging me tells me otherwise. You're much softer than you want to admit, but I'll play along, I thought to myself.

We sat in that car for another fifteen minutes while he spoke such beautiful things over me. Once he leaned over and grabbed his collar shirt, I knew our time was coming to an end.

"Baby girl, my boy is going to make sure you make it back to the apartment safely. Do you need me to have anything for you to make you more comfortable while you're there?" he asked.

"I don't want to sound like I'm complaining," I started before he cut me off.

"I want to hear what you have to say. Don't apologize or try to soften the blow for me. Just give it to me straight," Patrick declared.

"The man who walked me over here stinks, so if he's expecting anything from me, he's going to have to bathe," I responded boldly.

"You got it," Patrick responded. "Anything else?"

A kiss. A hug. Can you tell me when I'm going to see you again? Will I be doing this forever? How exactly am I getting paid? I want to believe you got me, but what exactly does that mean? Can I ask you for cash? Do I submit bills to you? How exactly is this arrangement supposed to work?

I had a million questions, but instead, I just kept them to myself and decided to ask for his help on something else.

"Well," I started as I adjusted myself in my seat. "This is going to sound crazy as hell, but I need advice. My mother has been pretending to be Latina because she wants to impress Delino. Before his daughter showed up, it was super easy to play along. Now, my sisters are worried because his daughter has been talking to someone who can blow our cover. I don't really know what to do."

In hindsight, I realize it wasn't safe to tell Patrick, but I found comfort in knowing he was too busy to be worried about the activities of some random junkie and her obsession with a man who would never want her.

"You're right. That shit does sound crazy as hell," Patrick responded before falling into a fit of laughter. Once he calmed down, he continued. "Listen, it is no one's place to judge how your mom lives her life, but that shit was funny as hell. Anyway, I wouldn't sweat it too much." He said casually as he poured us another round of shots."

"I wish I could laugh it off like you can," I responded somberly as I took the shot glass from his large hands. "My mother would kill me if anyone found out." I let out a deep sigh before I threw my head back to allow the warm alcohol a chance to numb all the anxiousness brewing in the pit of my stomach.

"Tell the broad the truth first. Find a way to make it seem dark and intimate. Then, make it seem like it's life and death for her to keep your secret. If she's a dirty bitch, you can try to make it seem like she's crazy since you didn't tell her the whole truth. If she's not, then you can gain some leverage with your mom when she thinks that you are trying to build a relationship with the bitch."

At that moment, it felt like a lightbulb went off in my mind. Then, as soon as it came on, it went dark as I started thinking of all of the ways the plan could fail.

No one is going to take my word over hers. She's basically royalty in these streets. How do I even set up the vibe to talk about something intimate with a broad that I barely know? I know for a fact I can't relate to this bitch.

My face must have given me away because Patrick managed to pull me out of deep thought. "You're gonna be alright, Tanya," he said confidently. "I'm taking all of the money that you're earning, and I'm flipping it to help put us in a different position. Whenever you need something, just let me know."

"So, if I needed a new place to live, what would you do?" I immediately spat back.

"Get you a spot," Patrick responded while looking deep into my eyes. "Anything else?"

For the first time in my life, I was sitting in a new emotion that I had never experienced before. As corny as it sounds, that shit felt magical. I decided that the hope Patrick had ignited in my spirit was not worth complicating the moment with any more questions.

"No, sir." I responded with a smile.

"That's my girl."

4

ELITE LIFESTYLE MANAGEMENT LLC

I had only been sucking dick for a couple of days, but I was quickly growing tired of it.

To break up the routine, I decided to ask the rich bitch to join me while I ran some errands. I was sick of living in fear about what the crazy old lady would tell Tammy. I was going to try Patrick's advice for myself.

Despite spending time together, I really had no idea what kind of girl she was, so I decided to bring her into my world.

The Book Trap was a small gem located a few blocks over from Tammy's house, so it was our first stop of the day.

I wasn't sure how she was going to respond, but I figured this was the best way to be vulnerable enough to share anything with her.

"Yo," Tammy exclaimed as she noticed the small table honoring the books that were written by Afro-Latino writers. "This spot is dope. I never struck you as someone who would be interested in books," she stated as she picked up a book to admire. I watched as she did everything I do when I see a novel I like. First, she ran her hands across the lettering of the hardcover. Then she opened it and began sniffing the pages.

Damn. I never met anyone who admires books the way that I do.

"Books are the only way I can escape the bullshit I have to deal with," I answered honestly as I found the poetry book I was looking for. To my luck, it was the very last one.

"Not Another Angry Black Woman," Tammy stated as she pointed out the book I had been eager to read. "It was amazing."

"You read poetry?" I asked as I looked over in her direction. "I would have thought that this kind of shit would have been boring to you."

"Real talk," she started as she picked up another book to admire. "Poetry was my first love."

I watched her crack a small smile as her eyes quickly glanced over the words on the page.

"Mine too," I responded as I shifted my attention to looking for another book. "In a perfect world, I would be able to create my own poetry books for others to read."

"Why don't you pursue it?" Tammy asked as she put the book down and transferred all her attention to me.

I don't have the money.

I don't know what I'm doing.

I don't think anyone would honestly care enough to read what the hell I have to say.

I think it would be a waste of time.

Long story short—I don't think anyone cares enough about me to want to hear my story.

"Yeah, right," I spat back as I continued browsing the book section we were in. "That's only for a certain group of people, and I'm not one of them."

"Bitch, that's bullshit," Tammy retorted as she walked over to me. Her energy demanded my undivided attention. "You can publish a book. I'll help you."

Why would you want to help me, I thought to myself as I scanned her eager eyes, hoping for some sort of answer behind them.

"All you have to do is prepare the manuscript, and I'll get it published," Tammy continued.

Unable to hold back my thoughts, I responded. "Just leave it alone. Some women are born with the world at their fingertips—like you. Then, there are bitches like me. I'll probably spend the rest of my life trying to get by."

They say the truth will set you free. Well, the honesty behind those words made me want to say fuck the rest of the day and just hide in my bed until tomorrow. Unfortunately for me, that would never be an option.

"I don't have the life you think I do," Tammy responded as she turned her face to find something else to look at. If Tammy had been anyone else, I would have assumed she was getting ready to cry.

I truly wanted to have sympathy for her, but then I quickly remembered that she has rich with parents who genuinely loved her.

She already has all that life has to offer. The last thing she would need is sympathy from me.

"I want to feel bad for you," I said as I cut through the awkward silence.

"Don't worry," Tammy responded as she turned away from me completely. "Most people don't feel bad for me. They don't care to hear about my struggles because I'm supposed to be good, right? The outside world sees a girl with the universe in her lap, but if you ask me, I'm just a prisoner trapped until I'm not."

Because her back was turned, it was hard to tell if she was crying. Judging from the way her voice trailed at the end of her last sentence, she was trying to avoid it.

"I don't mean to be funny," I spoke up softly as I stepped closer to her. "But how exactly are you a prisoner?"

To my surprise, Tammy turned around, with tears in her eyes, and passionately spoke up, "I just want to write. In my perfect world, I would travel the world, spreading my poetry. I would release a new collection every year, and I would share the parts of me that I hide from everyone but I can't."

Tammy was clearly ready to crack. It was obvious now that this girl had been holding this shit in for a while.

"My mom hates me. Even though I have access to endless amounts of money to fund any dream I could ever have, my mother chooses to shit on the only thing I want most. My father, who is still madly in love with her, will only do the things that please her.

"That means that I'll only get access to money if I become a lawyer like my mother wants or find a business opportunity my father can't refuse. Sadly, because he doesn't know anyone who has ever been successful selling books, he won't even hear me out."

Tammy hung her head low, allowing the tears she was fighting back to flow freely.

"My bad about all of this weird shit," Tammy said in between sobs. "I don't usually have anyone to talk to about this kind of shit. I didn't mean to throw it on you like this."

For the first time since meeting her, I didn't see her as Tamia Santiago—the heiress to a billion-dollar empire. Instead, she looked more like... me. Someone who was heavily misinterpreted and just learned how to be her own hero, so she didn't have to allow anyone the space to disappoint her.

"How can I hear some of this poetry?" I asked before I gently laid my hand on her shoulder.

***

I'm normally not a judgmental person, but there was nothing special about Tammy's apartment. I had always imagined a staircase of gold or a fountain of chocolate. Shit, at this point, I would have settled for matching furniture. She didn't live with any of that shit.

As if it couldn't get any worse, Tammy was sleeping in the same size bed I slept in. I was shocked. Granted, her house was clean, and everything they had was nice, but it was not at all what I would have imagined.

"Here it is," Tammy said with a smile as she grabbed her leather notebook out of her carry-on bag. "I haven't had the chance to write much since I've been here, but this is kind of cool."

I watched as she scanned a few pages before arriving at the poem she wanted to share.

"Don't judge me," she prefaced as she put the book down to look me directly in my eyes. "It's crazy because I've just recently started writing poems about love, so this is new for me."

Tammy closed her eyes. She took a deep breath, and then she began,

"I'm loving the way that loving you makes me feel.
I'm usually not the girl that's going to get wrapped or trapped by
her feelings, but the things that you evoke can't be avoided or
ignored anymore.
I can write novellas about the thoughts that bloom from the seeds
we've planted.
Your garden has become my safe space
A Holy place
Where I've seen miracles and God's grace
His patience is manifested by the way you aren't easily provoked

to frustration.
Instead, through conversation and your imagination
Your communication leads to revelation and liberation
Your demonstration of self-control is a solid foundation I want
my growing seed to see as they grow.
The organic way you flow speaks to my anxieties – silencing them
just by the way you move,"

Tammy shut her notebook. "I don't think this one is quite finished yet, but that's what I have for now."

"Damn, girl. That was dope as hell. I love the way you paint a picture with your words. I just want to know one thing. What nigga got you out here this open? I could never imagine liking someone enough to write something like that. Let me find out that Derrick is worth all these females gassing him up."

Tammy fell into a fit of laughter, and I immediately joined in. "Bitch, not a single soul I've ever encountered has given me the vibe to write something like that," Tammy spoke up once she finally caught her breath. "I think I'm just trying to speak him into existence with my words first—I guess. That's corny, right?"

"Nah. That's smart, actually," I responded as I tried to think about how I would even start a poem like that. "It's really talented that you can write something off of an emotion that you haven't felt yet."

"Thanks," Tammy responded with a smile. "Anyway, now it's your turn to share something."

Tammy's dedication to writing a poem through her hope gave me the push I needed to make the move I was there to make.

"I can share something," I started as I tried to adjust myself on her bed. "But your piece just inspired me to do something crazy as hell."

Tammy's eyes grew wide as she sat up. "What are you thinking of doing?" she asked.

"Well… this is going to sound crazy as hell, but I think I'm going to expose my truth in a poem. Even though I have a Spanish ass name— I'm not Latino at all."

Although Tammy never moved a muscle, you could clearly see that her eagerness had turned into confusion.

"I'm not sure how any of that is crazy," Tammy said. "Did I miss something?"

"Yes." I started as I grabbed her arms in an effort to be as dramatic as possible. "But you have to promise that you'll never say a word to anyone else about this."

"I promise," Tammy declared.

"My mother is madly in love with your dad. She thinks that your dad only dates Latin women, so she's devised an entire life that she thinks will fit into what he likes. That's why she gave my sisters and me the names we have."

Before I could finish the rest of my story, Tammy started laughing uncontrollably.

"I'm not laughing at you, girl," Tammy struggled to say as she continued laughing. "This just sounds crazy."

"Imagine how I feel," I stated as I allowed my frustration to step in. "My life isn't my own because my mom thinks that one day she'll have a chance with him. If she were to find out that I told anyone I wasn't Latin, she would kick me out and probably disown me."

Tammy took a second to really digest what Tanya was sharing with her. While the shock was funny, Tammy knew the struggles of having to live with a mother that you don't think loves you.

"I'm sorry," Tammy said after her laughter ceased. "I didn't realize how serious the topic was until you told me the whole story."

For a minute, we sat there awkwardly because neither of us knew how to continue.

I was stunned. Because while I was acting during parts of my confession, it required a lot of vulnerability from me. The truth is, I don't know Tammy or Patrick. Tammy could be the kind of bitch to say one thing in my face and then turn around and do something else. On the other hand, Patrick doesn't have all the answers to life. What if he gave me terrible advice?

"If you want to tell your story, I'll support you," Tammy stated as she broke the silence first. "But I really think we could both use this to our advantage."

I lifted my head and locked eyes with her.

"Even though I'm fully Honduran, I don't speak Spanish. That means I'm always in this weird little category of my own. I'm not 'black enough' for one group, and I'm not 'Latin enough' for the other side. I'll teach you some things so your act will be more believable, and we can just exist in our own lane together." Tammy suggested.

Truthfully, I wasn't sure how to respond. On one hand, it kind of sounded like she wanted to be friends—for real.

"Well," Tammy continued as she obviously grew tired of waiting for my answer.

Deciding to continue with this newfound vulnerability, I decided to boldly carry on the rest of the conversation with her.

"Are you trying to be real deal friends, or am I just helping you put on an act?" I asked her.

"You seem cool," Tammy responded. "But I don't know you enough to call you my friend. I'm open to kicking it more often once my dad slows down with all of the family he wants me to visit while I'm here for the summer."

"Perfect," I responded. "I know some bomb ass open mic spots that we can check out."

***

After that day with Tammy, we were together all the time. I took her to a few shows, and she took me around all of her primos (cousins). Lino, as he asked me to call him, even put another twin size bed in her room so I would have my own place to be comfortable. Of course, it didn't match anything inside of the crib. Still, I had a place where I could peacefully rest my head. For the first time in my life, I didn't feel so alone and on my own.

Tammy helped put some cash in my pockets by giving me a fee for every hair client that I booked. I kept her busy on the days she wanted to work, and she kept me paid.

Even though I knew she had to go back to Orlando when the summer was over, I got so used to being around her that it really hurt me when I had to take her back to JFK airport.

Mami is going to be so proud of me. I know how to make some of her dad's favorite recipes. Tammy taught me how to dance the punta, and I saw that Hispanic families are close as hell. Mami has to be proud of me now.

Sadly, my hope for a welcoming return didn't last long.

"Bitch, where the fuck have you been?" my mother screamed as soon as I walked through the door.

"Mami, I've been hanging out with Tammy and Lino," I responded in confusion.

Before I had a chance to realize what was happening, something hit me in the face.

I wish I could graphically tell you guys the details of my mother hitting me in the face with a plate before she lost it on me. I only remember two things: the taste of the soap suds in my mouth and the heat of the plate that had been soaking in hot water.

"Daydreaming of brighter days and getaways
Instead, I'm left scheming about how I can run away.
My mother hates me no matter what I do or say
That's why I'm seconds away from my villain stage
Cause I'm hurt and filled with fucking rage
I'm tired of having to jump on everyone's fucking page
Cause they don't care about me or my fucking wages
This world is cold
And it don't hold
A home for a bitch like me.
So I'm always the outcast,
Ready to outlast
Anyone ready to fuck with me."

I spit some of my best rhymes that day. It was the only way I was going to survive the beating that my mom put on me without swinging back.

To this day, I'm not sure what prompted my mother's response to me spending so much time with Tammy that summer; however, it was enough to get me desperate enough to reach out to Patrick to see if sucking some dick was still an option.

During my time with Tammy, I didn't care to reach out to Patrick to check on the money that I had made or to see if he had anything for me to do. We didn't have any formal arrangement, so I didn't see the need. That was a big mistake.

The next morning, I did my best to hide my bruises with the cheap department store makeup I had stolen a few months prior. I threw on a pair of sweats and made my way to the only place I knew to reach him.

Thanks to my time working with Tammy, I had a few dollars in my pocket so I could afford a drink when I strolled into the bar that Patrick frequented.

I looked around and was saddened to see that Patrick nor his entourage was there yet. I decided to sit at the bar to kill some time, hoping that he would eventually show up.

Two hours passed before the bartender decided to crush my hope.

"They haven't been coming in here," he said as he wiped down the section in front of me. "If you are sitting around waiting for them, you may want to hang it up."

I heard every word he said, but my brain couldn't afford to believe him right now.

If Patrick hasn't been coming around, how can I contact him? I know the money I made wasn't shit, but the nigga was willing to help me out of my shit. What the hell am I supposed to do now?

"How do I get in contact with him then?" I asked as I leaned in closer to the bar.

"That's between you and him, but I didn't feel right charging you for another drink without letting you know," he responded without offering up any kind of eye contact.

I paid my tab and left. Walking away without any clue of how to get in contact with Patrick Bennett made my situation feel even worse than it already was.

I know what you're thinking. I could have just asked Derrick. Well, while that is true, at the time, my mind wasn't thinking rationally. As I write this in retrospect, I could have casually asked that nigga to put me back in contact with Patrick. Instead, I decided to just pop up at the address that he previously gave to me.

I knocked three times—in the middle of the day. Then, when I wasn't sure if I was heard or not, I decided to keep knocking.

"Yo," I hollered, hoping to get someone's attention that was inside of the apartment. "It's me, Tanya."

For a moment, I tried to put my ear up against the door to see if I could hear any movement from inside the apartment.

Even though I didn't hear anything, I decided to keep knocking anyway.

This time, after my third knock, a burly black man flung the door open and snatched me inside the small apartment that I had only ever seen in the middle of the night.

For a place that was frequently visited by the city's hottest ballers and hustlers, the small apartment looked like the set of a cheap ass porn scene. There was a couch and loveseat and a small table with two chairs on the other end.

"What the fuck do you want?" the man asked once we were securely inside.

"I was hoping to find Patrick," I said as I made eye contact with a man who had been sitting in the cut with the largest weapon I had ever seen.

"You're a crazy ass broad," the man with the gun spoke up before he let out a heartfelt chuckle. "If you were trying to die today, I promise you could have found a safer way to do it."

The other three people in the room laughed at the man's comment. All of them were beautiful women who were all wearing next to nothing. By the looks of things, it looks like Patrick was getting ready to set up a night of easy money for the ladies sitting in his living room.

"Normally, Patrick would have specific instructions on how to handle a crazy bitch like you," the man who answered the door continued while the room once again chuckled at the comment. "After you just showed up at the bar and then you just popped up at one of his locations uninvited, you usually get the memo to not do this shit ever again."

The women looked around as the room grew more tense than it had been just a few moments before.

"Sit your ass down," the man continued. "I guess Patrick has plans to deal with you himself."

I wasn't afraid of anything other than my mami before that big-ass nigga made that comment. After watching the women scoot in closer together and start telling secrets, I knew that the nervousness I was already feeling was only about to get worse.

I had been sitting there for almost four hours. My stomach was empty as shit. My throat was parched as fuck, and my anxiety was beginning to turn into annoyance.

In the time that I had been waiting, three other beautiful women had arrived. Of course, none of them acted like I did when I got here. Nevertheless, the fact that the room was beginning to fill with more people gave me hope that I wouldn't be waiting much longer.

Just as I was beginning to get restless, I heard another knock on the door. This time, the man I was waiting for walked through it looking like a regular ass nigga. He was wearing a construction shirt and some gray sweatpants – nothing you would imagine a rich nigga to be caught dead wearing.

"You summoned me?" Patrick asked after he walked in and dapped his boys up.

Like always, Patrick's energy felt safe and scary at the same time. I wanted to hug him and find peace with the relief that he was easier to find than I thought, but I was also too stunned to speak. At that moment, I did the only thing my body would allow me to do naturally. I giggled.

"What's so funny?" Patrick asked. "I would love to find the humor in how you disappeared when you were working on a plan to get you out of your mother's house. Now, you want me to jump up and match your vitality? You're delusional as fuck."

Patrick always spoke harshly and to the point, so it made it impossible to read how I should respond next.

"I took your advice," was all I managed to say before Patrick cut me off.

"I'm tired of dealing with you entitled ass bitches," he responded. "You only want to do shit when it's convenient for you."

Suddenly, any excitement I had about seeing him vanished from my body. I felt embarrassed and humiliated while he continued with his rant about me being lazy and full of excuses.

I looked around and the other women in the room were all staring at me. Some of them wore looks of disgust, and the other ones had eyes of pity. Their looks were the most concerning.

I had heard worse statements about myself from the woman who birthed me, so Patrick's comments felt like child's play, but the women staring at me with concern in their eyes were all branded with bruises of different sizes on their bodies.

At that moment, I wanted more than anything for my mind to disengage with the rest of my body. I tried to think of my best poem starters hoping for a thought that would ignite an idea that would allow me to escape my present reality.

Your essence used to provide solace and hope.
If I had said I'm sorry would that have changed anything?
Why am I the answer to every problem in my life?
I fell in love with the devil himself.
I keep running with no destination in sight. This illusion that if I keep moving...

I made every attempt I could to mentally get out of that small room that suddenly felt suffocating and cold, but nothing worked.

Patrick continued with his rant until after he rolled himself a blunt. I watched as he finally shut the fuck up so that he could inhale the smoke.

God, please let this end peacefully and soon, I prayed as I hoped he found a moment of relief with that hit. As if my prayers had made it first class to God's ears, he spoke again with a different tone.

"I don't have to help you, so I won't," Patrick declared. "You can leave now."

While I was excited that the verbal beating was over, I still couldn't afford to leave there without a plan. Thanks to the soreness my body was feeling from the night before, I was prepared to beg this man for another chance to get some money.

"I'm sorry, Patrick. I won't just disappear like that again, but I'm ready to get back to work," I spoke, barely above a whisper.

"What the fuck did I just say?" Patrick roared. The smoke escaping his nostrils as he spoke made it all even scarier.

"Please," I responded. "I'm desperate. I have no one else to help me," I continued as I pushed back despite all of my fears.

The glare from his eyes confirmed I had every reason to be scared, but for the first time ever, I was more afraid of who I would have to return home to.

My mother had managed to break something in me the night before, and even though I couldn't pinpoint what it was, I just knew that her home could not be considered a haven for me—not for another day. I needed a new plan—fast.

I scanned the room again as I watched the women, hoping their body language would offer up some hope, but it didn't. Now, all of the women seemed to be locked into Patrick and terrified.

'Please, Patrick," I spoke up again. "I'll do whatever I have to do, but I need your help."

Patrick laughed before he took another long hit.

"Bitch, does this look like a charity organization to you? I'm running a business, and I can't do shit with a bitch who only wants to work when it's convenient for her. You know what I'm saying? How would that look to everyone else if I let them think you can be in and out like I'm running a burger joint?"

All of the women in the room let out a little chuckle. While I had heard a different variation of his joke before, nothing about it seemed funny from where I was sitting.

"This won't happen again," I responded, hoping he could hear my sincerity and desperation.

"You're right because I will never allow you to be this close to me again. Now, if one of these bitches in here wants to be your savior tonight, then that's on them." Patrick took a seat and took another long, hard hit.

Again, I desperately scanned the room. This time, I had been searching for a set of eyes that would allow me the chance I would have killed for. In a last-ditch effort for help, I removed my hoodie so the women in the room could see the fresh bruises from the beating I had taken the night before.

My world was already cold, so I wasn't expecting much. I grew up hearing that no one cares about your sob story. That's why I usually just suffered in silence, but for the first time in my life, I was willing to try anything else.

My body was covered in fresh bruises and cigarette burns. Every inch of my body hurt, and now I was suddenly scared of the whole world around me.

The eyes starting back at me all had different expressions, but none of them looked like women that were willing to help me. Just as I was about to put my hoodie back on and leave, a woman I had never seen before walked in the door and took control of the entire room.

"What the fuck is going on in here?" the woman asked as she looked around at everyone. "Why is this poor girl just standing here like this?" The woman walked over to me and gently laid her hand on my shoulder. I didn't realize it until she had touched me, but my body was shaking like a leaf.

"Girl, let me help you out," the beautiful woman said as she guided me towards the bathroom. Once we were inside and she had closed the door, I let out a deep sigh of relief.

"My name is Josie. I'm sorry about my brother," she continued as she took a washcloth out of the bathroom closet. "As you can see, he takes his Elite Lifestyle Management business just a little too seriously. This motherfucker really thinks he's out here running stables of bitches."

I wanted to laugh at her obvious attempt to lighten the mood, but the thought of Patrick hearing me was too much for me to deal with. Instead, I just gave her a small smile.

"What's your name?" the woman asked as she ran the washcloth under some warm water.

As much as I wanted to answer her, I couldn't find the strength to open my mouth. Maybe it was the warmth in her tone or maybe it was because this felt as close to a motherly interaction as I had ever received, but instead of answering her question, I started crying like a newborn baby.

To my surprise, the sweet woman pulled me in for an embrace, and I allowed myself to melt right in her arms as my tears flowed freely. I cried for every time I wanted a hug, but I knew I didn't have anyone to give me one. I cried for the times I just wanted to feel safe and seen, and this stranger left room to hold all the baggage that I dumped on to her.

"I don't know what you are going through," the sweet woman said softly as she caressed my back. "But I can promise you that it is going to be okay. You will be okay."

5

WHAT'S THE PLAN?

Josie Bennett was my saving grace that day. She helped clean me up in that dingy bathroom before she convinced Patrick to let me keep working. Although he was completely against it because of the show I had put on, she told him that I could do everything directly through her so he wouldn't have to worry about another pop-up visit like that, and he went for it.

While I wasn't excited to be sucking dick again, I was just glad to know that I wasn't alone with my plans on escaping my mother's house. I started picking up different events and dancing because I was tired of making small money. After seeing the money the women in that room were making, I knew I had to step my game up if I was going to be able to stand on my own two feet in New York.

For over a year, I put in work hustling all the money that I could get. Patrick and I both agreed that he should hold it for me. I even asked him to flip some of my money so that I would be able to ball out when Tammy moved back to New York the following year.

Every Sunday, after I was finished working, Patrick would slide me a twenty-dollar bill so that I would have my own money for food during the week. He taught me the importance of creating a budget, so I learned how to make that little bit stretch.

"Yo," Patrick said one night as he peeled out a crisp twenty from the wad of cash he had in his hands. "What's the plan? Are you just going to keep working and never get your spot?"

While I had been dreaming about the day when he initiated the conversation about me getting my own place, I was hoping that he would have been the one to secure a place for me. Since I was still a minor, I didn't know how to get a place in my name without Patrick finding out about my secret.

"I'm just saving for what I really want," I lied as I stretched my hand out to grab my money for the week.

"Damn bitch," Patrick started as he pulled the money outside of my reach. "What are you saving for – a penthouse? I thought you needed to get out of your mom's shit?"

"I do," I responded, unsure of how to continue this conversation. "I've just been working so much it's like I'm barely there anyway. I just want to make sure I'm smart about my next move."

That wasn't a lie. The truth of my reality was hard for me to swallow most days. I didn't have a plan on how I was going to make any kind of money without Patrick's support and connections. I had to be able to survive until Tammy got back and we could begin to take our plan to the next level.

Even though she was back home with her family in Florida, Tammy and I had everything outlined for our publishing company and the first few books we planned to put out. **Planet Fierce** was going to be the first Afro-Latina-owned publishing house, and we were going to help poets everywhere tell their stories to the world.

"Even though I'm not sure why I fuck with you," Patrick started, "You better be glad I do. Next weekend, I'm going to Magic City. One of my niggas is having a big ass birthday bash, so I'm bringing a few bitches."

My eyes grew wide at the thought of being able to hang around some real ballers. I had seen some of the women I had been working alongside cashing out on some real money. I was ready to get it all for myself.

For a moment, I allowed myself to get lost in the idea of owning a penthouse and having so much money that I wouldn't have to tolerate anyone's disrespect ever again.

While I've never been pressed to have designer things, it was only because I never had that as an option. Now, that shit was about to change.

I watched as Patrick's lips kept moving, but my mind was only focused on all the money that I was getting ready to make. I was so deep in my daydream I never heard when Felicia brought her hating ass into the apartment.

"I love to talk about money," the bitch started as soon as she was within eyeshot. "So, when are we leaving for Magic City, Daddy," she asked Patrick seductively.

"Bitch don't patronize me," he responded with a sly smile on his face. Like always, Patrick was hard to read.

"Tanya," Felicia continued as she addressed me directly since the first time I met her. "Next year, you'll be old enough for the out-of-state trips like the rest of us. Do you think your mom will sign your permission slip in the meantime?"

I didn't know how the fuck to respond. From the corner of my eyes, it didn't look like Patrick was even paying attention, so I decided to ignore her comment and slide out. I stood to my feet, and that was as far as I got before my dreams shattered in front of me.

"Answer her question," Patrick demanded. I quickly scanned him over, hoping for a sign that he was joking. Unfortunately for me, I knew better.

"I don't know," I lied. "That bitch doesn't even know me to make those kinds of assumptions so loudly." I did my best to stay calm. My girl Tammy taught me that it is important to control every square inch of your body when you are in the middle of a lie because if you aren't careful, your body language will say more than your mouth. Taking a page out of her book, I did my best to control my breathing. Even though anxiety was beginning to take over, I never removed my gaze from Patrick's direction, and I didn't give in to my body's impulse to wear the truth that I was doing my best to hide.

When I started working with Patrick, I was told never to tell him how old I really was. I always assumed it was because he held some code of ethics or some spiritual belief that he honored. After working with him for so long, it was obvious that Patrick only worshipped and respected money. Even though I wanted to believe that my real age wouldn't be a problem, I didn't want to cause any issues with Derrick since he put me in contact with Patrick. That's why I was determined to do my best to take my secret to the grave.

"Bitch, don't play with me," Patrick started as he stood to his feet and began walking in my direction. "What is she talking about, Tanya?" he asked again. This time, it was clear as day. There was no hiding his real emotion. The rage he was feeling could immediately be felt by the death glare he wore on his face.

I was too scared to mentally escape from that space, so I had to face him.

"Patrick," I started as I backed up a little bit. With nowhere else to go, I ended up falling back into my seat on the couch. If I wasn't scared before, the vulnerable position I now found myself in as he towered over my frail body took me over the edge. Suddenly, every ounce of confidence I had seemed to vanish.

"Answer the question, bitch," Patrick demanded again as he leaned in closer to my face.

"I don't know," I lied again as I tried to sink further into the couch. With both Felicia and Patrick guarding my only way of escape, I didn't know what else to do.

To my surprise, Patrick suddenly threw his head back in a fit of laughter. After working with him for a minute, I learned almost all of his different little laughs. I had never experienced this one before.

I removed my left hand that I was using to cover my face so that I could see what could possibly be funny to him at that moment. That was a big mistake.

The last thing I saw before I caught an open slap to the face was Felicia smirking at me.

You stupid bitch, I wanted to scream back. I wanted to tell her that I knew her delusional ass really thought she was Patrick's girlfriend, but I knew better. The force behind that one slap hurt more than anything my mother had ever done, and I didn't want to experience it again.

I grabbed my face in agony, afraid of what I was going to see when I looked in the mirror.

"Don't worry," Patrick started as he used his other hand to rub the hand he had just slapped me with. "You're not going to bruise, but you may need something to help with that blood."

Just as the words left his lips, I began to taste blood filling my mouth. I looked around, hoping to find something so I could avoid making a mess. I didn't want to have a reason to upset him any more than he obviously was. With nothing around to help, I chose to swallow the warm, metallic-tasting liquid.

"Nasty Bitch," Felicia stated with a smirk as she stood over me with her arms folded. "At least now we know that there isn't a liquid you won't swallow."

I pray that I never get this desperate for love and attention that I behave like this fucking bird, I prayed as I looked up at her with hate in my heart. I had only met Felicia a handful of times, but each time was the same. She always spent so much of her energy trying to show that there was a clear difference between how Patrick treated her and the rest of the women he worked with. She would stir the pot and cause drama, but this was low—even for her.

"How old are you, Tanya?" Patrick asked as he lifted his hand again.

At that moment, I cracked. Every plan I had to hold down the truth crumbled as the fear of another slap took over. "I'm seventeen," I stated between sobs.

I had my hands in front of my face, but between my fingers, I could see Patrick stepping back in disbelief. Patrick's tough exterior came down for the first time ever, and I briefly saw a scared little boy trapped in a grown man's body.

I looked over at Felicia as she wore a smile of pride. While every opportunity I had to get on my feet was ruined, this raggedy bitch was celebrating my agony. Does she think I enjoy this? Unlike her, I wasn't doing this to try to impress Patrick. Every move I made with him was to get me away from my abusive ass mother. She sucked dick, hoping the money she made would impress Patrick. We could never be the same.

"Get out," Patrick demanded. "And don't you ever come around me or any of my people *ever* again."

What about my money?

What about my place?

What about my future?

I wanted to ask him so many questions, but I knew that now wasn't a good time.

But if I don't ask him now, when will I get another opportunity?

I took a deep breath and tried to settle on a confident but not aggressive tone before I spoke up. "I'm sorry," I started. "I'll just take what I've earned and…" was all I could say before Patrick fell into another fit of laughter.

"What money have you earned?" was all I heard Patrick say before I drowned him out with my thoughts. While he went on and on about how easily he could take my *worthless* life, I allowed my mind to finish a poem that Tammy had been struggling to finish.

"I realize that taking care of my mental should be primero – pero – yo necesito dinero," Tammy stated one day before we both fell into a fit of laughter as she attempted to write a poem in Spanglish.

Wanting to escape that room, finishing my girl's poem felt too easy.

I realize that taking care of my mental should be primero
Pero
Yo necesito dinero
In this world where money is the driving force
Striving for both, mi vida takes its course
Love don't pay the bills
And these niggas don't either.
These desperate bitches out here lack faith, so I'm gone make them a believer.
Watch me get this bag
And have all of the things they said I would never have
Yo queiro cribs, cars, and to live like movie stars.
And I'm gonna do it.
Soy loca
Y
Mi boca
Y
Chocha
Es
Fuego
Might have some screws loose but
The extra lack
Helps me not take any slack
From these pendejos
I'm on their necks
I'm on the grind
And I'm coming for everything that's mine.
And it's only a matter of time
Before you all see: the world is mine.

I was mad comfy in my flow when the danger in Patrick's voice brought me back to reality.

"Be glad I'm letting you leave with your life. Consider whatever money I was holding for you a down payment on the money you owe me for this treason."

6

AND JUST LIKE THAT...

And just like that, I was back to square one. Fortunately for me, I had learned to live off half of what Patrick used to give me a week, so I had a little change hidden away. While it wasn't a lot, it was going to help me buy some time until Tammy moved back. I only had a couple more months to go, so I still had a glimmer of hope to hold on to.

"This is the most I've seen your ass in over a year," Nina stated as we sat on the stoop instead of being crammed in the house. "You aight?"

For a second, it almost sounded like my sister had real concern for me, but I knew better. They were always on my side until it was time to stand up to Mami. Then, both of my so-called sisters couldn't wait to throw my ass under the bus.

"Yeah, I'm good," I lied while doing my best to hide the tears that wanted to fall at that moment. "I was out here chasing dreams for a little while, but they didn't lead anywhere in the long run.

That last part was sadly the truth. Even though I had done some of the nastiest and most vile things alive just to try to survive, I had nothing to show for it.

"Cut the small talk," Tiffany started as she stood up. "Tell us about all of these niggas you've been fucking with. Don't act like the streets don't talk, bitch."

Fuck.

I knew I would have to face the music eventually, but I never planned on it being like this. I always imagined my family finding out after I had so much money and power that they wouldn't give a fuck about how I got it all.

"Niggas lie on their dick every day, B," I responded hoping she would just crack a joke and move around. I wasn't in the mood to talk about anything that was going to remind me of Patrick or anyone I met while I was working for him.

"Well, then I need you to clear up the rumors," Tiffany continued. "Suddenly, you have a little change to spare, and these niggas are saying some wild shit, so make it make sense for me."

I did my best to avoid looking at my sister while she asked for me to give information that I just wasn't ready to share yet. Then, for the first time in my life, my mother came up like an answer to a prayer.

"I hope my house is clean," Mami stated as she pushed past me on the step. "You bitches been home all day, so it better not smell like pussy up there."

I watched as my two sisters straightened up their posture and put on the fakest smiles I had ever seen.

"You play too much, Ma," Nina said as she let out a false chuckle. "But everything is good up there."

"Good," my mother continued as she dug through her bag to grab a cigarette. "My future husband is supposed to be coming over tonight, so we can talk about the details of his daughter moving back."

For the first time since my mom walked up, I sat up in excitement. The thought of Tammy returning to New York for good was definitely the answer to all of my problems. I knew that once she returned home, I wouldn't have to spend so much time at my mother's house, and I definitely wouldn't have to answer my sister's silly questions about the strange things I did for change. After all, something about Tammy's demeanor wasn't very inviting, so most people weren't going toe to toe with her. In the wrong instance that someone would try it, all she had to do was flash a sly grin. There was something about seeing her smile when nothing was funny that struck fear in the hearts of some of the toughest people I've met.

"What did he say about her coming back?" I asked—speaking up for the first time since my mother got home.

"Wouldn't you like to know?" Mami asked as she turned and glared straight into my eyes. Maybe it was the fact that she was standing over me, or maybe it was how quickly I had managed to change her energy, but I suddenly didn't want the answer anymore. In fact, I immediately regretted allowing my curiosity and joy to speak up for me just moments before.

The rebel inside of me thought of so many clever things I could say in response to her question. *Maybe if I come in hot, she'll back down.* I briefly reasoned with myself before settling the issue by flashing her a little grin.

I wasn't in the mood to fight. I was tired, and I had only asked my mom in hopes that Mr. Santiago had a trick up his sleeve. I was hoping that he could provide more hope than the conversations Tammy and I had daily about our future plans.

"Bitch, as soon as I land, we need to hit the ground running with these plans," Tammy would declare every time we shared a new poem with each other. And with our high school careers coming to an end, we knew our days of being boss bitches were close enough for us to taste it.

"What's funny?" Mami asked with a straight face, bringing me back to reality. "I want to laugh too."

I didn't have a response to her question. I only pulled a Tammy move, hoping it would have the same effect it always had with her. Usually, most people would change the subject. I should have known that I wasn't going to be that lucky.

The look in her eyes was enough to strike fear in my heart. *Would Mami beat me in broad daylight?* I wondered to myself as I quickly scanned my eyes to see who would witness the beating that was inevitably coming.

"Bitch, what the fuck is so funny?" Mami asked again. Only this time, you could feel the heat oozing from the words that came out of her mouth.

A part of me wanted to run, but I was all out of backup plans, so I had to do my best to stay quiet and out of the way until Tammy came back.

I was in a lose-lose situation, and I knew it. If I spoke up, she would find a reason to be offended. If I didn't respond, she would say I was disrespectful.

"I was just curious, Ma. I've been taking a lot of losses lately, and it would have been nice to have her around. That's all." At that moment, I decided to be fully transparent and honest with my feelings and emotions.

"Girl, please," my mom said before she started laughing. "Your dramatic ass is always going to try to manipulate yourself into being a victim, huh? Aren't you tired of that yet?"

I didn't respond, hoping it was a rhetorical question. Thankfully, it was.

"We discussed that when Tammy gets here in a couple of months, we don't want you living over there. It puts too much strain on our budding relationship," my mother said with a straight face as she searched for a cigarette in her purse.

Mr. Santiago would have never said that, I thought to myself as I remembered how accommodating he was the last time she was here. For a moment, I was tempted by the thought of asking my mom a follow-up question, but something deep inside me told me that it wasn't worth it.

She's just trying to bait you into a reason to beat your ass, I thought to myself.

"I don't want to repeat myself," my mother warned as she found what she was looking for. Make sure this is my only warning.

***

"We about to party and bullshit," I proudly sang out the lyrics to one of my favorite Biggie songs as Tammy and I walked back to my house to get ready to party that evening.

In the week leading up to Tammy's arrival, I felt every emotion except defeat and sadness. Getting to that moment had been a challenge, but I survived it. Now that my best friend and business partner was in the city for good, my mom would have to find a new scapegoat to take her self-hatred out on.

Just as we were reaching my building, Derrick pulled up on us out of nowhere.

"Damn, Tee! You come back, and you don't even holla at your boy?" Derrick asked.

Seriously, it was lowkey embarrassing to watch Derrick perform so poorly as he made his best attempt to connect with her.

"I only get to find shit out about you through your Myspace now," Derrick continued. "I see you're letting your online celebrity status get to your head.

I pretended to ignore them as my sisters and I continued on in front of them. It took everything in me to contain myself against Derrick's lack of spitting game. But I managed to remain quiet. Before he left, he made sure to let her know that he bought her something she would love.

"Damn bitch," Nina said once Derrick was no longer around. "What the fuck do you do to have Derrick and the rest of these niggas acting the way they do for you?" she continued.

"Don't gas her," I interjected before Tammy could reply. "It's not that hard, and it's nothing I couldn't show you if you were just willing to learn." I joked.

"Hoe, please," Nina replied with a laugh. "I was actually asking for you cause I was hoping you would take notes. Yeah, these niggas give you money and buy you shit, but you have to suck and fuck the whole crew for what you get. Once you do the math, you're not even making minimum wage," my sister said before they all exploded into a fit of laughter.

We've always been the type to roast each other from time to time, but considering what I just went through with Patrick, that shit hit different.

"Whatever," I huffed as I tried to play it off. "It really ain't that deep. Anyway, I like fucking and the power it gives me when I'm done with them," I snapped back, hoping to change the tone of the conversation.

"Well, actually," Tammy spoke up. "We as women have more power until we actually sleep with them."

I wanted to believe the truth in what Tammy was saying, but the girl was trying to act like we didn't talk on the phone every day. I watched my girl shoot her shot with love. I saw her attempt to settle down with the nigga she loved all throughout high school. Despite his attempt to lock her down, she wasn't going to commit to someone she couldn't trust.

"Fuck that shit," I responded. "I need to catch mines while putting a few dollas in my pocket. At least I'm not like you bitches that just fuck for free."

That part was true. My two sisters loved to act like I was crazy for being rumored with some of these niggas, but those bitches gave their cat away without as much as a fucking thank you.

We all got ready before my mom could ruin the vibe, and before we knew it, we were in the middle of a hood party having a ball.

Tammy was a bad bitch, and she was new to the city. We were not there long before niggas was in her face—pressing her. I was too busy trying to sell one of Tammy's services that I never noticed the guy that Tammy had been talking to.

"Do you know what the hell you just did?" I heard my sister ask Tammy with much concern in her voice. "That's Rasheeda's man, and that bitch is crazy as hell."

In true Tammy fashion, she played it off because she was only trying to get him to spend his money. Despite how crazy that hood rat Rasheeda is, the rest of the night went without incident. Well, that was until it was time to let out.

"So you want to fuck with my nigga?" Rasheeda yelled out angrily. I took a deep breath as she started talking all kinds of shit. I decided to sit back and watch how Tammy handled the situation.

True to her nature, she tried to resolve it quickly and quietly, but that was too much for a project chick like Rasheeda.

"Bitch," I growled as I stepped between Rasheeda attempting to charge Tammy. "If I have to tie my hair up, I'm going to beat your ass," I continued, meaning every word of it.

To my surprise, Rasheeda didn't want to take it much further than that. Instead, she gave Tammy one more glance over before she rounded up her clique and left.

After that incident, I could almost feel Tammy's bond change with me. I assume, from the stories that we shared with each other, that like me, she wasn't used to someone having her back. Well, she didn't know that I was prepared to always hold her down like that. After all, she was the one who exposed me to the idea that I could have hope for my situation.

To my surprise, Tammy never asked me to spend the night. She didn't attempt to make plans for the next day either. *Maybe my mother was telling the truth. Maybe her family doesn't want me around.*

"Thought you had a friend," my mother taunted as she tried to be funny.

Since Tammy returned, I only hid out in my room until my stomach demanded something to eat. I wanted to avoid dealing with my mother at all costs, but she was making it hard.

It must be miserable knowing that this is the highlight of her life. My mother spends most of her day gossiping and being a bitch. She doesn't even have hope for anything better than this for herself. I wonder which one of my sisters will be her next victim when she doesn't have me around to bully anymore. I watched on as my mother searched her bag for another cigarette while she sat in front of the TV. *How sad...*

I was halfway to the kitchen when I heard the buzz that let me know someone was downstairs trying to get our attention.

I ran over to the window and looked down, hoping to get a glimpse of who it could be. Knowing that would be the first thing I did, I watched as my best friend took a few steps back, looked directly at my living room window, and gave me a big smile. Without any hesitation, I let her in.

Fortunately for me, my mother never tried her shit whenever Tammy was around. That's why I loved having her here.

"You're such an asshole," Tiffany said when she finally stopped laughing at Tammy's story of her recent encounter with Derrick.

"Damn, so you finally let Derrick go back on the market?" I asked as my brain tried to plot a good excuse for me to reach out to Derrick. "That means he's free game since you clearly don't want him, right?"

I watched as she seemed to get a little uncomfortable with my bold questions before she responded.

"I never said I didn't want him in my corner anymore," Tammy responded. "I put him exactly where I wanted him."

While Tammy kept talking, I lowkey tuned her out. She had already given me the information I needed to make my next move. I now had a reason for Derrick to want to speak to me, but first, I would need his help retrieving my money back from Patrick.

7
F*CK NIGGAS – GET MONEY?

"Damn, you just went completely ghost," I stated, not bothering to mask my irritation. "I haven't seen your ass in over a month, and the crazy part about it is that you live just a few blocks over. What the fuck have you been up to?"

Truthfully, I was hurt. Tammy and I had spent years planning our time together when she moved back to the city, but she was not following through with any of it.

After my last night with Tammy, I put my plan in motion with Derrick. Everything started out smoothly. He had agreed to help get me back in contact with Patrick, but first, he wanted a chance to see Tammy and me together.

"I met someone," Tammy responded lovingly. "I've just been a little booed up and caught up with him."

"Hmm.." I responded. I'm sure my irritation was obvious as I unenthusiastically rolled my eyes. "That sounds a little too mushy coming from a female who proudly claims that she'll be forever mackin'. Who the hell are you, and what have you done with my friend?" I seriously wanted answers.

"Well, things change," Tammy responded in a matter-of-fact tone. "Aren't you happy for me?"

I couldn't believe what I was hearing. How had the woman who had aspirations for her own publishing house suddenly forget about everything because she had some nigga in her face?

"For what?" I asked irritably. "It will be over sooner or later. Then, you'll remember where your real friends are. A real relationship isn't your style. You've tried it before, and you always leave once shit starts to get too deep. You might be trying to play him, or you might be trying to play yourself. But you won't play me," I declared with a firm tone.

Sitting on the floor in my bedroom was not the place I imagined having this conversation, but Tammy had been hard to link up with these days.

"Damn, you sound like a real hater, Tanya," my sister Tiffany spoke up. "If a man can get Tamia Santiago to settle down, gush over him, and go ghost on her friends, he has to be special. Doesn't that mean something to you as her homegirl?"

Truthfully, I wanted to smack fire from my sister, but I was a woman on a mission. I didn't have the time or energy to feed into whatever she was talking about.

"Settle down my ass," I replied. "She is going to do his ass just like she's done everyone else she's ever been with. You know she is not letting go of any of her hoes just for one nigga. You all can play along with her and her foolishness, but I'm not buying it. Not even for a second.

"Speaking of your hoes," I continued as I tried to change the direction of our conversation. "Derrick has been desperately trying to get in contact with you. That nigga has even had his boy passing messages to me to try to get in with your ass. His boy just told me that D has been leaving all kinds of gifts, flowers, and shit at your pop's house. So, I guess you were right; your plan actually did work."

I watched her body language, hoping for a sign that I could get those two in contact. She didn't offer up anything.

"Fuck Derrick and that plan," Tammy responded. "I'm not even worried about all of that. I took a really long vacation, but now it's time to get back to the money. That girl Rasheeda has been keeping my calendar filled with all types of bitches wanting to get hooked up, and I put it off way too long.

Thanks to my dad, my beauty line will be out in the next few months, and it's time to just remind everyone that when it comes to anything beauty, Tamia Santiago is where it's at. I don't want to hear any more bullshit about Derrick or any of my old hoes. I just want to make my money and deal with my boo," Tammy declared.

Listening to my homegirl list every plan and not include anything about the one we had been working on for years hurt. As if my sisters could feel my pain, we all, in unison, let out a resounding "Damn," once she was through outlining her plan. I listened on as my sisters tried to front like they were happy for her, but I couldn't believe everything I was hearing.

"Well, ya'll can play along, but I won't believe it until I see it myself," I spat back to the rest of the group.

"He's going to be at our spot on Friday with some of his niggas to play a few games of pool and for a few drinks if ya'll want to meet him," Tammy offered up.

"Well, I'm definitely going to be there too," I responded.

***

The few days leading up to that Friday evening felt like torture, but I was ready to get my plan in motion.

"Fuck men and all of their bullshit," Tammy stated somberly as Tammy, my sisters, and I all lifted our shot glasses for a toast. "From now on, it's fuck niggas – let's get this money."

Despite the words coming out of her mouth, it was easy to spot how bothered my homegirl was by the sudden change of plans. *Damn that nigga really got to her.*

We hadn't been there very long before the man I had been dying to see walked in with a group of his boys. Patrick Bennett was live and in the flesh. Tonight, I was ready to do more than sit around plotting my next move.

I played it cool for the rest of the night. That was until I noticed that he was walking over to our table.

Oh shit, I thought to myself. *Maybe he's ready to finally apologize for how he treated me.* I did my best to hide my excitement.

"Don't you have something to say to me?" Patrick stated bluntly as he fixed his watch.

I was shocked. My sisters didn't know I had any dealings with Patrick, so I definitely didn't expect him to be so public about everything.

I honestly didn't know how to respond, but before I could say a word, Tammy spoke up first.

"Yeah," she replied timidly. "Why don't we go somewhere more private and discuss this?"

"For what?" Patrick responded as he briefly cut his eyes at me before centering his gaze on her. "If you mean what you're about to say, then you won't have any issues saying it in front of anyone—and especially not your own friends."

I looked over at Tammy and watched as she gave him a soft glare. It was almost as if she were pleading with him through her eyes. I had never seen her respond to anyone like that—ever.

"Well," Patrick stated with a sly grin.

"I'm sorry, and you were right," Tammy stated. "Are you happy now?"

I couldn't believe it. The man who had my homegirl running around here acting like a love-struck puppy was none other than Patrick Bennett.

"That wasn't so hard," Patrick laughed as he extended his hand out to grab Tammy's.

"I'll catch up with you bitches later," Tammy said with a smile after she put a crisp hundred-dollar bill on the table.

I watched in horror as she grabbed his hand and slid out of the booth.

"So much for fuck men," I yelled out before they left.

***

For days, I tried to pretend like I wasn't bothered by how Patrick Bennett managed to fuck me over again. Without knowing it, he weaseled his way into the heart of the only person I ever had on this earth.

During my time with him, Patrick had put me on to a lot of game. That's why I knew I couldn't just tell Tammy the truth about Patrick. No. She was going to have to find out for herself.

In my desperation, I reached out to the one woman who had always been ready to help me in the past when it came to him. I knew that it was a risky move, but I was desperate.

After a few weeks, I finally had everything in motion.

"Hmm," I said with an attitude as Tammy sat down to join me for lunch at our favorite sports bar. "You love pulling this disappearing act on me so often now. I never know when you'll just go ghost on a bitch anymore."

I had so much more I wanted to say to my girl. I wanted to ask her if he was making her do anything she was uncomfortable with. I wanted to know if they started making money together, and more importantly, I wanted to make sure that he was not doing anything to hurt her.

"Relax, Tanya," Tammy responded. "Your time is going to come, boo. One day you'll find love and know exactly why I'm acting the way that I have been lately." The large smile Tammy boasted made me sick. Not because I didn't want to see her happy, but because I knew the real version of the enemy she was sleeping with.

"I would pump by brakes if I were you talking about all of that love shit because there are a lot of things you don't know about your so-called lover boy."

I did my best to remain calm, but I was fuming inside. I had read about the poems and love stories my friend was dreaming about. There is no way she knew about Felicia or the other bitches fighting for Patrick's attention.

"Well, obviously," Tammy responded while not removing her eyes from the menu she was looking over. "There is also a lot that I don't know about you, but you don't see me giving you shit every damn day."

No, she didn't, I thought to myself. How could she ever say something like that when I've been around and holding her down? Patrick just came up out of the blue.

"You are about to be under a lot of stress, so I'm going to let that foolishness slide," I said in a matter-of-fact tone.

"Excuse you?" Tammy responded, not bothering to hide her annoyance. I watched as she laid her menu down and leaned closer to the table. "Was that supposed to be a threat or something?"

Why is this bitch suddenly acting like she doesn't know me?

"Bitch, please. If I was going to fuck you up, I wouldn't warn you. I'm really trying to help your unappreciative ass out if you would shut up and listen." I took a deep breath and continued. Lying to Tammy was not going to be an easy thing to do. "Get this, I was super curious about your boy, and after you left, I did a little digging around on him for you. Don't worry, you can thank me later.

"Anyway, that woman by the bar in the red dress can tell you everything you need to know about this nigga that has you acting funny," I stated as I cut my eyes in the direction the woman was standing in.

I cut my eyes over to the bar where Josie Bennett was sitting. While I wasn't proud of myself for lying to Tammy like this, I knew that she deserved to know more about Patrick. My problem? I had to make her want to seek more information.

"The woman at the bar's name is Josie," I said when I peeped that Tammy wasn't as eager to the conversation as I had hoped she would be. "She's the mother of his kids and his live-in wife," I lied.

I watched as Tammy's steady and calm demeanor transformed. I could almost feel her heart rate increase by the way her breathing changed from my last statement.

While it hurt me to be the source of pain for Tammy, I knew that I needed to protect my friend no matter what.

8
NOW WHAT?

Watching Tammy run out of our spot in tears that day was rough, but it needed to be done.

Since then, we still were not hanging out like we used to, but I knew it was a matter of time before we started working on our publishing company again.

"Have you worked on any new poems?" I asked Tammy while she went on a scribble spree in her black leather notebook.

"Nope," she responded flatly.

Since the other night, Tammy had been impossible to break through to.

"Come on, Tee," I pleaded as I closed my notebook. "This isn't like you at all."

She didn't immediately respond. Instead, I watched as she glided her pen across the cream paper. She sat hunched over, with her legs outstretched and her notebook in her lap. At first glance, you could see that a brush had not touched her curly hair for at least a week. And although she didn't smell bad, she didn't smell good either.

"Bitch, what do you want me to do?" Tammy asked while she continued on with her doodles. "My dad won't give me a break from this fucking makeup company. I can't tell if it's my shit or his at this point. Now... this nigga..."

Tammy lowered her head a little more.

This nigga is trash.

This nigga is a cold-hearted bastard who only cares about himself.

This nigga is never going to do right by you.

This nigga has mad bitches who would cause you problems if they knew about you. I thought to myself as I did my best to ignore the rest of my racing thoughts.

Sitting there, leaving room for my girl to feel all those emotions, wasn't easy. I wanted to tell her the truth about the man that she fell in love with, but I knew better. I had seen far too many episodes of Jerry Springer and Ricky Lake to know that getting in between relationships was only going to bring more drama.

"Tammy, I know this seems hard, but you deserve better than him anyway. Look at you. You aren't even acting like yourself with this guy. Don't you want someone who is going to be the guy you've been writing about in your poems?"

For a brief second, it looked like Tammy attempted to smile.

"I never told you I finished that first love poem I read to you, huh?" she asked as she changed the direction of our conversation.

I watched as she searched through her notebook, looking for the piece she was ready to recite.

"I'm loving the way that loving you makes me feel.
I'm usually not the girl that's going to get wrapped or trapped by her feelings, but the things that you evoke can't be avoided or ignored anymore.
I can write novellas about the thoughts that bloom from the seeds we've planted.
Your garden has become my safe space
A Holy place
Where I've seen miracles and God's grace
His patience is manifested by the way you aren't easily provoked to frustration.
Instead through conversation and your imagination
Your communication leads to revelation and liberation
Your demonstration of self-control is a solid foundation I want my growing seed to see as they grow.
The organic way you flow speaks to my anxieties – silencing them just by the way you move
You walk in sync with consideration
Always including thoughts of me before you step.

What more can I ask for?
A decisive man
Who intentionally created a space for me and all my baggage
One who knows my bad habits
Yet only speaks to the leader in me.

Baby, it feels like that man was created *only* for me,
So how could I not love the way that man makes me feel?

"Does that nigga got a brother," I asked playfully. "Because I'm trying to see something."

We both took a moment to laugh at my lame ass joke.

"Can you honestly say that the nigga you are sick over right now is anything like that man you wrote about in your poem?" I asked her once the laughter stopped.

Without any hesitation, my dawg shook her head, "No." "Bitch, you're right," Tammy said as she sat up and snapped out of it. "Let's organize this poetry book."

***

"I can't do this," Tammy cried out while we sat in a plush hotel suite in Manhattan.

"My life changed overnight, and I don't know what to focus on next."

Shortly after we settled on our first manuscript, Delino, Tammy's father, was murdered. Then, everything changed.

With my mom's dream man dead, she made it obvious that she didn't need me around anymore. Mr. Santiago was barely in the ground before my shit was sitting on the stoop.

Because Tammy had just inherited her father's finances and problems, I hadn't seen much of her lately. In fact, it had been months since I laid my eyes on her. I was surprised when she called me inviting me for a quick getaway.

Seeing my girl like that was hard because I had no idea how to support her. With everything she had going on, all I could do was offer help.

"There is one thing you can do for me," Tammy said once her tears subsided. "I need your help setting up this nigga who is trying to come for me now."

I scanned her face, hoping to find a hint that she was only telling a joke. I didn't find anything.

"We're not those kinds of broads, Tee," I tried to reason with her while I checked just how serious she was.

"Well, I am now," she responded with a level of confidence that I hadn't seen her with in a minute.

Did I want to set someone up? Obviously not, but what other choice did I have? I was tired of sleeping at some random jump-off's crib to have a place to lay my head for the night. I didn't feel right asking Tammy about our publishing company, so I just decided to follow her flow for now.

9
BYE FELICIA

Tammy didn't give me all of the details of the mission. Originally, all I was told was that some nigga Brian needed to be handled before he caused any more problems. That was before I knew Patrick would be involved. Then, I spent my days leading up to the robbery learning everything I could about our mark.

Patrick Bennett had managed to weasel his way back in by warning Tammy that Brian was out to get her. Well, turns out, that was a big fucking lie. Apparently, Brian and Patrick were in a war and Patrick had been ducking and dodging this man by staying in different hotels all over the East Coast for years! You see, Brian is everything that Patrick wishes he could be. That's why Patrick decided to use Tammy to lure Brian into his territory. Sneaky right?

Anyway, the night we robbed him changed my life. That was the first time I was given access to real money. That night we ended up counting so much money, my fingers began to change colors from touching all of those bills.

For the first time ever, I was confident that I wouldn't need the help of another soul to fund my dreams. Planet Fierce was going to be a publishing house that would change the game for black girls who wanted to tell their stories to the world, and I was going to do it without needing anything else from anyone else.

"I'm proud of you, mama, but we got another nigga we need to get," Tammy declared as she passed me the blunt she was smoking.

Oh, hell no! I thought to myself as I tried to calculate how many sleepless nights I suffered through just to arrive at this moment. Tammy and I laughed about how much I obviously wasn't built to do this shit in the long run. Why would she ever think I would be okay with doing this again? She might enjoy the fast money, but I was ready to take my twenty bands and create a new way of life for a lot of bitches like me.

I cut my eye at Tammy, hoping that she would get the hint. Instead, the Grim Reaper spoke up to add his two cents before she could respond.

"Plans change all the time, B," he stated before erupting in a fit of laughter. "I'm sure you know all about that," he continued once he caught his breath.

It took everything in me not to curse him out. As much as I wanted to go off on him for changing our original plans, I knew if I did, I would be giving him exactly what he wanted. Instead, I simply ignored his ass.

Again, I scanned Tammy's face, trying to reason and plead with her. As much as I wanted to stand up for myself, I didn't have the energy to go through all of that with Lucifer present.

"This nigga killed my pops," Tammy stated as she looked me dead in my eyes. Her piercing gaze and the reason behind the next mission told me that, once again, my dream of my own publishing company was going to have to be on hold.

"You don't have to explain yourself to her," Beelzebub spoke up again, obviously trying to piss me off.

"Excuse me, sir," I responded as I turned in my chair to face in his direction. "I'm trying to have a personal conversation with my best friend. If you wouldn't mind, can you please keep your commentary to yourself? We got this."

I looked over in Tammy's direction to check her body language. Because she had been on edge since I walked in, she was already too hard to read, but the glare behind her eyes reminded me of the face she made when she realized that she had to take over her father's drug dynasty.

Unlike the first time I was met with this expression, I knew I now had the power to do something to help her. Despite my initial reservation, I now felt like I had to do something.

I knew that the Antichrist was going to think that he won this round, but I didn't care. My girl was going to need someone in her corner, and I knew better than to trust the tongue of the nigga she was sleeping with.

Without any other choice, I decided to honor the vow we made years ago when we were younger. I was going to do whatever I could to help hold my girl down.

"What's the plan, mama?"

10

PLAY NO GAMES

The original plan was simple, but since I know that some of ya'll need more background knowledge, let me tell you a little bit about this nigga Jason.

Jason Thompson is Tammy's right-hand man because when Delino was alive, he watched over Tammy and the rest of her family. Oh, he's also best friends with Patrick Bennett. Messy as fuck. I know.

Anyway, back to what I was saying. Jason had moved to Orlando because Tammy had created a little sting operation to catch another nigga named Scheme. While Jason was in the middle of his mission, Derrick, who went into hiding after Delino was murdered, showed up and told Jason about the bitch that murdered Delino. As soon as Tammy got the information, she immediately told Jason, who we also call Beast, that they were about to kill two birds with one stone. While he worked his way to get Scheme to trust him, she also wanted him to become another nigga's plug.

Kyle Cole, also known as K.Y. in the streets, was a small-time hustler. He was also the only person who had any way to help us locate his mother, the woman who was supposedly responsible for taking out the biggest King Pin on the East Coast.

Listen, I'm about to speed through this information to get you all caught up with everyone else, so keep up. K.Y. fell for the bait. Between Jason's prices and the fact that it aligned him with Tammy, that nigga fell head over heels in love with her. Then, she used Kyle's street cred to solidify her way into a meeting with Scheme. Why was this guy so important? Well, it's because his uncle, Lorenzo, faked his death years prior when the FBI was closing in on him. Lorenzo and Tammy's grandmother, Estrella, were soulmates, and Tammy was determined to reunite the two lovers. But she knew that a nigga like Scheme was going to be wary of letting go of such a big secret, so she created a big-ass illusion until she got what she wanted out of him. Not only did my bitch get the info she wanted from both of them niggas, but she also managed to find herself in a position where both of them wanted to lock her down in love.

Damn. Giving you all the cliff notes version really puts into perspective why some people call her shit a "hood novella." Anyway, because I had helped her with both operations, I was able to see through all of the bullshit. While I do believe Kyle has real feelings for my girl, I know that he isn't man enough to handle her for real. He was a young, small-time drug dealer before my bitch elevated him in business. Regardless, he fell in love with a watered-down version of Tamia, so I knew that he wouldn't be able to handle her once he got down to her roots. I did everything I could to keep them apart because, from the moment I met Scheme, I knew that he provided the kind of love that my best friend deserved to have.

Luckily for ya'll, the love story between Tammy and Scheme is still being told, so if you want to know more about them, all you have to do is **Charge It to the Game**, and wait for the next part of her story to come out. Kyle, on the other hand, will have his chance completely revoked once Tammy reads this and finds out that I succeeded in getting him to sleep with me. Once she finds that out, Kyle is out of here.

As I bring this little story to a close, I realize that it's hard to fight back some of the tears that suddenly need to flow. Looking at my words on paper brought me to a brand new revelation. If I am unsuccessful in getting Patrick to admit on camera to some of the things that Tammy doesn't know about, my life will never be the same again.

Regardless of what happens next, Tammy, I need you - specifically - to know the truth. Regardless of the picture I intentionally painted, I've always had your back. Shit is about to hit the fan, and it's important that you know that I've done all of this to protect you.

One night, after a night of crazy sex, Detective Harris confessed that he was getting desperate in his attempts to take you down. Because I allowed him and everyone around us to believe that I didn't love you as much as I do, he became really comfortable telling me inside shit. That nigga told me that a correctional officer in some jail in Florida had enough evidence to sit you and your entire organization down forever. It didn't take me long to find out the officer he was talking about was none other than Felicia Robinson, Patrick's bottom bitch of almost a quarter of a century!

I'll be honest, bitch. I don't know what she knows about you or anything going on with any of your businesses. All I know is that she will do anything for Patrick's love and affection. I mean, she really did waste her prime time years and then some fucking and sucking every nigga she could. The crazy heifer really thought that because she was his cash cow and the bitch who tolerated everything, he was going to choose her when he settled down. Can you believe her?

Anyway, shit is about to go down if she starts singing because she would only do something like this out of desperation. Because a nigga like Patrick can't afford anyone who even thinks about involving the feds, Felicia has gone rogue. She's either desperate for Patrick or fed up with his shit and is ready to take him down. Either way, you'll be caught up in the crossfire since you are the closest thing to him.

Oh, let's not forget about all of the consequences that came your way because of Patrick's selfish desire to involve you in a *war* between him and his enemy, Brian. He *used* you and fed you to *wolves* for his own personal gain. Then, wasn't even around to help you pick up the pieces of the mess.

Tamia Santiago, I love you girl. That love for you caused me to play some parts I never imagined playing, but I always did what I could to protect you.

I'm glad I got the chance to write my story, afterall. I still don't give a damn what anyone else thinks about me as long as you know the truth.

And for anyone else who is reading this shit that is not Tammy, you better make sure she gets this, or I'll haunt you forever.

BOO BITCH.

No. Seriously, please make sure my bitch gets this. Then, I want you to take a few hours and put your own story down on paper. I didn't realize how therapeutic this was going to be until I got to the very end, and the tears started flowing. I now get why people tell you to take control of your story and tell it yourself. If you continue to let niggas play in your face and stay quiet about it, they'll tell everyone who will listen that you enjoyed it—or whatever Zora Neal Hurston said.

COMING SOON:

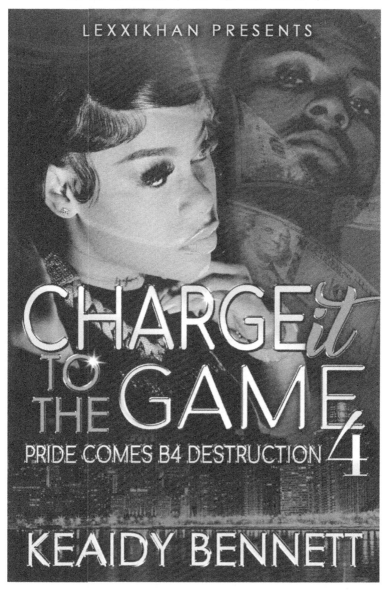

LEXXIKHAN PRESENTS

CHARGE it TO THE GAME 4

PRIDE COMES B4 DESTRUCTION

KEAIDY BENNETT

Continue reading for a snippet from the highly anticipated fourth installment of the **Charge it to the Game** series by Keaidy Bennett.

Charge it to the Game: Pride Comes B4 Destruction
BY: KEAIDY BENNETT

"Kenya," Amethyst shouted from the presidential suite of the hotel they were in. "He's dead!"

Kenya Cole stopped in her tracks as she spun around, dropping all of the weed that she planned to roll into a blunt.

Please be joking. Please let this be a cruel prank, Kenya thought to herself as she did her best to remain calm.

"What the fuck do you mean he's dead," Kenya responded barely above a whisper. "We've been doing this too long, and we are too good at what we do," Kenya continued as she tried to convince herself to remain cool. "How much of that shit did you give him?"

"Bitch, I gave him the same amount that you showed me," Amethyst responded as she started talking a mile a minute. "Or maybe I didn't. I think maybe I just had way too much to drink tonight. Shit, maybe I'm just losing touch with my game. I don't know, girl, but I don't think I made a mistake.

Kenya wanted to run, hide, and scream. The last thing she wanted to do was be in a room with a dead man that she had planned on extorting for money. She could see it now – her face plastered on every tabloid for being the hooker responsible for murdering a powerful and wealthy man.

Think bitch, Kenya thought to herself as she briefly scanned over the room. *We can fix this. We just have to slow down these thoughts and figure it all out.*

"Can't that Tee girl help us out," Amethyst spoke up, interrupting

154

Kenya's thoughts. "What was her name again? Tina? Talia," she continued as she went on to mention every female name that started with a T.

Fuck! This is exactly why Tammy told me not to give Amethyst any information on her. This just went from bad to worse.

"Tanya," Kenya asked, hoping to deter her friend from probing any further.

"Yeah! Where is that bitch at? I'm sure she can help us with this mess. Maybe we should reach out to her."

Shit, I seriously wish I could call Tammy. She would know exactly what to do right now.

"How the hell would I be able to call her," Kenya spoke up. "We aren't supposed to have our phones on us, remember?"

The look on Amethyst's face told Kenya everything that she needed to know. Amethyst had foolishly broken their biggest rule. Because of the advancements in technology, they knew that allowing their phones to ping off the same towers as one of their victims was not something they needed to be doing.

"I'm so sorry, Ken," Amethyst spoke up. "We've just been doing this shit for a minute, so I got a little sloppy this time."

Unable to hold back anymore, Kenya took a deep breath, grabbed one of the pillows from the couch she was sitting in, and screamed into it.

"I know it looks bad now, girl, but maybe this was to help us out. You can log in to your social media from my account, and we can get Tanya to help us out of this mess."

It took every bone in Kenya's body not to slap her friend and tell her the truth. If Tammy had her way, Amethyst wouldn't have been anywhere near Kenya in the first place. Instead, Kenya would have been some square-ass college student trying to chase a career instead of this quick illegal money.

Tammy has been telling me to watch out with Amethyst. Why would she bring her phone the one night that this suddenly happens?

Wait…is he actually dead, or is she just trying to set me up so that she can gain access to my social media? Thanks to my time at the strip club, I have some of the world's most successful men following me and in my DMs.

"I need time to think," Kenya stated as she did her best to mask her irritation. "What are we going to tell detectives when they see that we were in a hotel room with a dead man while we just browsed social media? We have to think smarter than this."

Hold on to her phone. You don't know how much you can actually trust her right now, Kenya thought to herself.

"You stay trying to make shit harder than it needs to be," Amethyst spat back. "For all you know, Tanya could have a connect in this fucking hotel that could do the work for us. Why do we need to sit here and struggle if we don't have to?"

On one hand, she does have a point. Tammy always has a trick or two up her sleeves. It wouldn't be uncommon for her to have a connection in a fancy ass place like this. On another note, what if Amethyst planned this, and she's trying to set us both up to take the fall?

"You don't know her like I know her," I responded as I started to pace back and forth. "I don't think Tee is going to help me out of this one."

"Bitch, please! Tee has been bailing you out of shit since before I even knew you," Amethyst responded.

She wasn't lying. Kenya's life immediately changed the day she met Tamia Santiago. Before her, Kenya saw herself as just some book-smart girl who did what she was told. Tammy taught her how to be her own boss and survive on her own terms.

In fact, Kenya had spent so much time around Tammy that she eventually started to move just like her. Shit, Tammy got so worried that the way Kenya was moving was going to change her, she even offered Kenya enough money to start over far – far away from this shit. Unfortunately for Kenya, she fell in love with the fast life and fast money.

Only a few minutes had passed since Amethyst announced the dead rich guy lying on the floor of the hotel that was booked in his name. Kenya's breathing had returned to a normal pace, but her mind refused to slow down.

Tammy would have never allowed herself to end up in this situation, Kenya thought to herself. *She is way too smooth and calculated to get caught up in bullshit.*

I wonder what she's doing right now. Maybe it wouldn't hurt to give her a call after all...

***

"Let's go, Santiago," the guard yelled as he unlocked Tamia Santiago's cell door. "It's time to get you in population."

"Population," Tamia Santiago asked as she stood to her feet. "There has to be some kind of mistake. I'm not even supposed to be here. I didn't do anything. I haven't talked to my lawyer, and Detective Harris still hasn't talked to me since arresting me. What the hell is going on?"

"Listen, princess," the guard responded. "I know you're used to calling all of the shots out in the streets, but in here, you do what I tell you to do. All of that other shit isn't any of my business. My job is to get you in an orange jumpsuit and out of these holding cells. Now, let's go."

Tammy was furious. At that moment, all she wanted to do was scream, cry, and hit the guard in his face, but she knew that it would just make everything worse. She felt her anxiety climbing and figured that it would be in her best interest to follow him because she wasn't going to talk herself out of this one.

If one of those bitches try me, she thought as she followed him down the poorly lit hallway. *I'm going to destroy them. No,* another thought interjected. *That would just add on to whatever Detective Harris is holding me for. I don't want to get any more time than he's trying to give me now. I can't mess this up. I can't let my emotions get the best of me. I can't do time in jail – I'm not built for this. I can't freak out now. I just can't fall apart. God, please help me keep it all together.*

Luckily for Tammy, they reached their destination before she had a chance to fall any deeper in thought than she had already been.

"Here," he said as he passed her two sets of orange jump suits, a pair of slides, and a bag with her pillow and bed linen. "In the bag, you'll also find a bar of soap, a toothbrush, and toothpaste. On Wednesdays, we give you an hour in the library. It was that little room we passed just before getting in here. On Sundays, you can go to church in the morning if you want. You just have to make sure to sign up for it. If you need anything else, like lotion, socks, or underwear, you're going to have to pay for it out of your commissary money.

Once you're done changing, I'll take you to go meet your new roommates."

Tammy turned to go change in the small bathroom. Even though she wasn't going to avoid going to population, she took her time to for every step. She wanted to enjoy the last minute of peace and solitude she had remaining. Tammy was afraid of the uncertainty of what was coming next. Were the girls going to be cool and funny like they were on Orange is the New Black, or were they in search of their new top dog like in Wentworth? For the first time in her life, Tammy was finally ready to go in search of the woman she really was and not the person everyone thought she should be, so it was depressing to know that she would have to play another part just to survive.

Who is the jail house version of Tamia Santiago? Is she a bitch? Does she fight and curse a lot more than usual? Is she peaceful and calm like the Muslim niggas in all of the urban fiction books? God, please help me, she prayed out again.

In that moment, Tammy realized that she had prayed more since having those cold cuffs slapped on her wrist than she's ever done in her life. *Is this a part of the Tammy I have to be in jail? Does she pray a lot and rely on God more?*

"Let's go Santiago," the guard called out. "I got other shit to do today."

Although she was already dressed, she couldn't bring herself to open the door. She wasn't ready to find out what jail was really like. She had always imagined that she was too good to get caught slipping. Honestly, she never considered that she would ever end up in jail. Sure, she always preached about it when trying to get other people around her to do right, but she just never thought she would be here.

"Give me one minute," she cried out as she tried to buy herself more time. "I'm almost done," she lied.

"No, you're not," he screamed back. "I can hear you pacing around in those cheap ass jail slides, so I know you're already dressed. Get out here."

Damn. How the fuck am I going to survive in here playing any kind of part if this nigga can catch me slipping so early? God, I know I don't really fuck with you like that. Wait, can I curse when I pray? I mean, I feel like the bible says to come as I am, and I curse, so that's cool, right? Anyway, I need you to help me through this. I know I've said in the past that I would change if you helped me out, but I really mean it this time. If you'll get me through this, then I'm going to do something different with my life. I can't make any promises like I would preach like my cousin, but I will try to be a better human. Please just help me through this.

"Ok," she called back to him. "But can we please stop by the library first? I know it's not Wednesday, but I've never had to do this before, and I think having the chance to read a book will really help me out. I know you technically don't have to do anything but your job, but I would really appreciate it," she pleaded.

"If you get your ass out of there in the next ten seconds, I'll take you."

Tammy took a deep breath and quickly grabbed her things.

"Who knew that a trip to the library could make a woman move so fast," he chuckled.

For the first time since being arrested, Tammy let out a soft laugh herself.

"I just really like books. I wish I would have listened to my grandmother and focused more on my poetry and writing than I did doing other shit. I know if anything is going to help me out, getting the chance to read a good book will help."

She followed the guard as he walked her back through the hallway to the small library. When he opened the door, she was disgusted to see the way the books were treated. There was no organization to what was there, and from what she could tell, there weren't a lot of selections that she really wanted to read.

"I see mad bibles and ripped up magazines, but where are the good urban fiction novels or some poetry or something," she asked as she skimmed through the books that were there.

"Look, the warden is really picky about what kind of books are allowed in here. Anyway, you just said you need to be more focused on your writing and shit, right? Why not take the time to do that? Here," he said as he passed her a stack with a few sheets of blank paper and three small pencils that didn't have erasers. "I know it's not a lot, but it's a couple of the items we give you guys in here. That should be enough to at least get you started."

"You know," she said as she took the stuff he was giving her and placed them in her mesh bag. "Ya'll guards aren't as bad as they make ya'll seem on TV. You seem pretty cool. What's your name anyway."

"C.O Mack and not everyone is relaxed. I'm just doing this while I finish school, so I do what is asked of me while trying to treat you guys like I would want someone treating me. Don't get it twisted, though. There are a lot of people in here looking for that next promotion, so they do everything by the fucking book."

Tammy had a million questions she wanted to ask, but she was terrified that he might know who she was or someone who was connected to her team. How would niggas on the outside want to work with her if they knew that jail time was so scary to her?

"Luckily for you, niggas is pretty chill in this unit. There is one chick, though, that they say is crazy. Apparently, she swallowed a battery so they could send her to psych. I guess her plan was to try to escape when she was in there since they aren't handcuffed, but it obviously didn't work out. Now, she just spends most of her time sleeping. The other girls you'll be locked down with just keep getting small time for petty shit. They don't start a lot of trouble cause they are just trying to get back out to their drugs. C.O Robinson is a bitch, so make sure you follow her instructions. Other than that, just try to lay low and write. Oh, make sure you write your books in the third person or something. You don't want anyone in here thinking you got a diary with confessions. Otherwise, those niggas will shake down your cell every damn day."

Shake down, she thought. *What the fuck is that? I thought that shit was just for T.V.* Tammy wanted to ask him, but she was so grateful that he started pouring out some of the information she needed. It offered her more relief to know what she was going to be facing when she got in there.

"Bet," she responded. "I really appreciate all of your hospitality C.O Mack, so I think I'm finally ready to go."

Even though the library wasn't very far from population, the journey felt treacherous to her. The sound of their footsteps echoed eerily off of the drab off-white walls while her mind kept rehearsing every possible worst-case scenario in her head.

"Ladies", C.O Mack called out as they approached population. "Your new roommate is here, so make sure you play nice."

He unlocked the large door, and Tammy followed him inside. Tammy wasn't sure what she had expected, but this definitely wasn't it. The room had two separate parts. On one side, there was a large table, one window, some chairs, and a television. The other room had four desks and two bunk beds that were all bolted to the ground.

"Hey! My name is Tina Brown," the youngest, most pale girl spoke as she jumped up. "Let me help you put on your bed linen. That fitted sheet is always the trickiest."

Tammy paused for a moment because she wasn't sure how to respond. On one hand, she appreciated the offer, but she had read enough urban fiction books to know that no one is ever really your friend in jail.

"First time," she asked when she noticed Tammy's hesitancy.

"Yeah," Tammy responded as she scanned the room for everyone's responses. She noticed the open bed that was probably hers. It was the one that was above a young woman sleeping soundly while everyone else watched.

"The first time is the hardest – especially if you don't know when you're getting out or what to expect in this process. I'm Christina Brown, by the way. I've been in and out of this place since I turned eighteen a few years ago."

Christina was a tiny thing. If she hadn't revealed that she was in her early twenties, Tammy would have assumed that she was too young to be locked up with grown women. She was only five feet tall and couldn't be any more than a hundred pounds. Her baby blue eyes were impossible to miss. Although she obviously needed dental work, her smile was so inviting. There was something about her that seemed genuine. Sadly, Tammy wasn't sure if she was able to trust that feeling because she had also felt the same way about meeting her old best friend, Tanya Isabella.

"Come on," she said as she took Tammy's bag to find the fitted sheet. "Lunch will be here soon, so let's get you settled. We usually go on lockdown after lunch, so you'll want to have it ready."

Because of some of the shows that Tammy had seen, a part of her felt like she couldn't let the other girls think she was soft. She had just allowed the smallest girl in the room to take her stuff from her after all. Again, she scanned the room to see everyone else's response. To her surprise, one of the other girls went back to reading her book. The other one got up, grabbed her stuff, and headed to the back of the room where the showers were.

Almost as if she had sensed what Tammy was thinking, Tina spoke up. "Being locked up here isn't as bad as being locked up in other places. Sure, there are some jails out there that I would have never tried to grab your stuff from you, but it's cool in here. A lot of the girls that end up in here don't have to do a lot of time, or they are on their way to prison, so it's not a lot of drama usually.

Anyway, can you share some stuff about you? What's your name? Why are you in here?"

"My name is Tammy, and I'm honestly not sure why I'm here. I was arrested and booked, but I never got the chance to get any information as to why I'm in here."

"They do that sometimes. That's their way of getting you to sweat it out. I wouldn't be surprised if they make you wait a few days before coming in here to have that conversation with you. This is their way to get you to think of every bad thing you've ever done in your life, so they can hopefully get a confession out of you. I don't like being in here, so I just hear whatever they tell me and then sign my little deal so I can go about my business."

"You know that's part of how they keep you in this system, right? Usually, a deal comes with probation or something, and their goal isn't for you to ever be off of that. They want you to end up right back in here," Tammy responded.

"Oh, you're one of those conspiracy theorists. You'll love Manda when she wakes up. She's always saying similar shit, but I just hate being in here. I wish I didn't do the things that land me here, but I can't help it. I like drugs, drinking, and partying, but it's always the reason I end up back in here. This time it was because I stole some shit to get some money. I wanted to get high, and money has been tight since my baby daddy won custody of the kids. After that, I just started partying harder cause when I'm high, I don't feel anything but happy. When I'm in here, I'm forced to think about shit soberly, and it sucks. Anyway," she said as she stood up. Judging from how much she struggled to get the sheet on, Tammy was glad that she decided to let her help. "Lunch is about to be coming up soon. During feeding time and when we have rec is the only time you'll see your bottom bunk roomie. Her name is Manda Santana. She's cool, but just don't fuck with her. She dated some drug dealer who got her strung out on heroin. Then, one day he, his money, and his drug supply vanished, so she had to learn the hard way that her habit wasn't easy to keep up with. She had a robbery ring operation going on for a while. They stole all kinds of shit. If you ask her where the money went, she'll tell you that it all went to drugs. Don't ask her about how much time she has, though, because it will just piss her off. The other girls and I think it's around 20 years, but don't trust us because we ain't lawyers," she giggled. "Adrianna is the Mexican girl, but we all just call her Ari," Tina nodded in the direction of the young girl who was reading to herself. "I don't know a lot about her because she doesn't talk about herself very much.

She'll join in with us during games or conversations, but that's about it. The dark-skinned girl is Keisha. For some reason, I'm just really afraid of her. But she's never done anything to me or any of the girls in here. I just feel like she would beat me up if I said something crazy because whenever we watch our ratchet reality shows, she always says, 'I'll beat dat bitch ass.' I believe she could really do it."

Just as she had finished her final sentence, Keisha walked out of the showers.

"Bitch, you in here talking about me again," she asked as she put her stuff down on her bed.

This is it, Tammy thought as she tensed up. *This will be my first real experience with jail life.*

"Yeah," she responded boldly. "I was just giving the new girl a little a little information about everyone she was locked up with."

Tammy noticed that Keisha relaxed a little bit as she grabbed her lotion. "Well bitch make sure you tell her that you like to run your fucking mouth too." Tina and Keisha both erupted in laughter.

"Like she said, I do like to run my mouth, but I won't do shit. I'm as scared as they come. At least I won't lie about it like other people. My mouth is crazy, but I'm not. I'll talk my shit, but I'll also stay in my corner."

All of the girls laughed at her honest confession.

"Inmates! It's lunchtime," Tammy heard as the large door swung open.

"This is C.O Robinson," Tina whispered to Tammy. "Do what she tells you – how she tells you to do it, and you can usually avoid a problem. I can't guarantee that it will because she is always searching for issues."

Since the first time Tammy had gotten to population, she saw Manda's face. She was beautiful and had rich chocolate skin. Judging from her hair texture, Tammy wanted to assume she was also an Afro Latina. Still, she knew better than to just assume.

"Listen," Manda said as she took her seat for lunch. "If any of ya'll don't want your food, I'll eat it."

"We know," Tina said as she sat across from her. "You say that at every meal because all you do is eat, shit, and sleep."

"So, we have fresh meat," C.O Robinson said as she handed Tammy her lunch.

She wasn't sure how to respond to her since she had heard so many rough things about her, so she chose to stay silent and just join the other girls.

"I'm guessing your mama never taught you anything about manners," she said as she began pouring their mandated eight ounces of milk. "Since you can't say thank you, I guess you don't need this either."

The part of Tammy that inherited her dad's dynasty wanted to fight for it, but a huge part of her didn't feel like it was worth it. At that moment, Tammy decided that this new role she was willing to play would choose peace over everything else. Instead of lashing out, like she would have in the past, Tammy chose to be silent.

At that moment, she thought of her grandmother, Estrella Cruz, and she found herself getting emotional.

Before eating, Tammy bowed her head and began to pray. *Fuck! Not now. I can't do this here, and I certainly can't do it in this exact moment. Everyone will think I'm soft as fuck, and this bitch will think she broke me down. Lord, if you will just get me through this moment, I promise I'll learn to be silent more.*

She knew she hadn't been praying very long, but Tammy was relieved to see that C.O. Robinson was gone.

"That's fucked up that she really didn't give you any milk," Manda said before she shoved her last spoonful of food in her mouth.

Nah. It's fucked up that they actually serve us this shit. Tammy used her spoon to move her mushy meal around her plate.

"If you don't eat now," Tina spoke up. "It will be hours before you get to eat again. The next meal isn't any better than this one. It will be two bologna and cheese sandwiches, a bag of chips, a banana, and a cup of milk. Well, that is if you don't manage to get under Robinson's skin again."

"I've been in this hell hole for a long ass time, and I've never seen her act that way with anyone before. Ya'll know each other on the outside or something," Manda asked.

"How can you ever see anything when you're always sleeping," Tina joked.

"Bitch, now is not the fucking time to pop off with your shit unless you want to get slapped too," Manda retorted.

Tina didn't respond. Instead, she used that as a moment to chug down her milk.

"Seriously yo, do you know her?"

"No, I don't," Tammy responded earnestly.

"You might not know her, but everyone knows who the fuck you are. That shy shit isn't going to work in here, and it's humorous that you want to act so holy." For the first time since Tammy arrived, Arianna spoke up.

Uh-oh.

"Clearly, you have an issue with me, so let's address it. What's up," Tammy asked.

"You killed my fucking brother, bitch!"

Tammy immediately saw the faces of the two young men she had murdered in her mind. She scanned her face expeditiously, searching for any trace that she might have been related to either of them. A part of Tammy knew that this could have been a trap, but a larger part of her was tired of carrying that secret for so long.

"Bitch, who the fuck is your brother," Keisha asked boldly.

"Francisco Gonzales and he was a great father and brother until he got hooked on the product that she's pumping in these streets. You think just because you have other people doing your dirty work that we didn't know you were the one responsible for so many deaths in our community. I hope they're charging you with every life you've ever fucked up."

Tammy was speechless.

"Now you want to be silent? Any other time, you would be out here calling shots and hiring hits, but now you want to be fucking quiet?"

"Look, Adrianna, I really don't know how to respond to you right now. Yes, I've made a lot of fucked up choices in my life," was all she was able to say before she was cut off.

"So you admit that you killed my brother?"

"I never said that. My terrible choices in life affected a lot of people. I'm genuinely sorry that any choice in my life had a negative impact on yours. I used to be selfish as fuck, so I never stopped to consider anyone else's feelings. I'm sorry for anything I did to you."

The room became jarringly silent.

Without finishing her food, Ari got up and went back to her bunk.

Manda immediately grabbed her plate.

Tammy had officially lost her appetite. She got up and went to get her stuff to take a shower.

Is this a safe decision right now? The bitch didn't respond and for all I know she's in here for battery or something. Tammy's mind began to race with all sorts of worst-case scenario situations. She decided not to let her thoughts control her.

The hot water felt refreshing on her skin. Although it was much hotter than she usually would have showered, she just enjoyed the peace that the solitude was providing her. It felt good to not have people blowing down her phone for everything. Even though she was in jail, a part of her felt relief from the pressures of just living her life.

More than anything, Tammy wanted to pull out a sheet of paper and one of those raggedy pencils to finally tell her story. Still, she remembered what C.O. Mack had warned her. The last thing she needed was a written confession to any crime – no matter how beautifully she would have written it.

After her shower, Tammy immediately went to her bed. All of the other ladies were sleeping, and Tammy felt like she could use a nap also.

Before she had a chance to fall into a deep sleep, she was jolted awake.

"Santiago, let's go. You've been summoned," C.O. Mack called out.

She sat up frightened. Luckily for her, none of the other girls were awake to see.

"Who is it," Tammy asked once they left earshot of the other girls.

"You're finally getting the conversation you wanted with Detective Harris."

Shit.

"I hear you've been pissing people off since you've been here. That was quick as fuck."

"Nah," Tammy responded. I literally didn't say a single word to her and she spazzed on me."

"I was just messing with you. She told the rest of us that you guys had some sort of issues outside of these walls."

"That's the thing – I honestly have no idea who she is. What kind of issues could we have?"

"Apparently you guys were sharing the same man."

Tammy laughed.

"That's impossible. The only nigga I rocked with would never rock with her."

"Well, if you let her tell it. You and sis was out here sharing that nigga Rick."

At that moment, it felt like her stomach had fallen and hit the ground. Sure, she said she wanted to move on to find herself without him, but she had loved that man more than anything at one point in her life. Hearing that hurt because in all of the years they had been together, she never once entertained the thought that he might have been unfaithful.

Before she could fully process all of her emotions, they arrived at the small interrogation room.

"You're always fly, but you look so much better in orange," Detective Harris spat as soon as she walked in the room.

"Detective Harris, do you mind explaining to me why the fuck I'm here," Tammy asked.

"Don't play dumb with me, Tee. There are a million reasons why you should be in that fucking jumper. I just finally got something that would stick."

"Well, do you mind sharing that with me? It would be really nice to know what the hell is going on."

She was having a hard time maintaining her confidence, but she managed to pull it together like she always did.

"Well, originally, I only planned to charge you for murder and first-degree arson. But you decided to leave me with no choice but to finish you off with the death of your frenemy, Isabella, or Tanya, or whatever the fuck her name is.

The jury is going to love making an example out of you. I can't wait to see their faces when they find out that you and a group of your employees set fire to a home. You knowingly planned the murder of Sasha Cole since you were upset about her killing your father. Once you found out that your best friend had turned and was acting as our intel, you had her murdered."

Tammy was numb. She promised Kyle that she wouldn't seek revenge. If she really was dead, would he ever believe she had nothing to do with it? Although Tanya Isabella had been a terrible friend to her, she just couldn't manage to forget all of the good times they had shared together. In her mind, their friendship was real; however, she was finding that the betrayal was starting to hurt worse than the loss of their friendship.

Ask for a lawyer.

"I don't know what you're talking about," Tammy responded emotionless.

"Of course, a real criminal never tells his dirt. You'll take all of your secrets to your grave, but you can bet that I will make you pay for every one that is exposed to me."

Say you want a lawyer.

"Let me guess, you're here to offer me a deal if I tell you what you want to know," she chuckled.

"Nah, love. Those offer days are over. I actually just came to gloat. It seems like every time I'm satisfied with the thought that I'm beating you, the universe just sends me something else to finish you off with."

Again, Tammy's stomach felt like it hit the floor. She was beginning to get nervous. Usually, Detective Harris was always on a mission to get her to talk.

Breathe. Relax. Don't let him see you sweat. Stop engaging with him and lawyer up!

"I really have no idea what you're talking about. I would have never killed Sasha Cole, and the last time I saw Isabella, she was alive and well. I think your obsession with proving yourself is starting to make you desperate." Despite her anxiousness overtaking her, Tammy sat back in her seat and relaxed.

"I've watched every minute of footage we have of you in here, and I haven't figured out how you ordered her hit, but I will figure it out. I can promise you that. I wonder how your baby will feel when he or she only knows you through prison bars."

"Baby," a confused Tammy responded. "Clearly, you have me mistaken for someone else.

Stop believing shit this man says. He's trying to get you to crack. Ask for a fucking lawyer.

"Every inmate is tested for shit when they come up in here. One of them is a pregnancy test. Congratulations, mom. I'm sure your child will have a promising life out there while you're in here."

What the fuck? Tammy wanted to scream. Sure, she told Patrick that she wanted kids, but she didn't expect any right now. She thought she was going to have time to clear up her life first. Afterall, she took her birth control religiously to avoid this moment. Her life was already fucked up, and she was trying to mess with anyone else's – especially not her own flesh and blood.

A part of her wanted to be happy about the news he had just given her, but with her future still hanging on by a thread, she knew now was not the time. What if Detective Harris was able to put her away for good? What would happen to her baby?

"From that puzzled look on your face, I'm guessing you didn't know," he sat down in the chair directly in front of her.

"Listen, Tee, there is no reason a child should be born into this mess. I have enough to put you away forever. Patrick is going to eventually slip up, and I'll get him too. Is this really what you want for your child? You don't have a good relationship with your mom. The only person who would have loved that child like you would is dead, and with both of its parents locked up, your little one will undoubtedly end up in the system too."

The thought of her grandmother not being here for this phase in her life made her want to cry immediately.

I already feel like I haven't been able to trust Rick for a minute. Now, this bitch is telling people she had my nigga — my child's father? What if he really has shit on me and can make it stick? Will this bitch be around my fucking baby? Will Patrick even keep it? Her thoughts were starting to get louder and louder. She watched on as Detective Harris' mouth kept moving, but she couldn't focus on anything other than the thoughts pounding loudly in her mind.

"Look," Detective Harris said as he slapped a heavy manila folder on the cold, metal table. "You can continue to play this tough guy role if you want, but everyone knows you aren't ready to serve no real time. Tell me what I need to know about Patrick and the rest of your team, and I'll work out something to allow you to be there for your kid. What's it gonna be?"

ABOUT NENSHIA DANIELS

Born in Jacksonville, FL in September 1990, Nenshia Daniels is a mother of two beautiful girls. Always having a love for literature, she began writing stories as a pastime and mental release from her academic workload while in college. That pastime accidently producing her entire book, Nenshia found that not just reading but writing was a part of her passion. Her imagination and descriptive writing style pulled the words from pages to visuals in readers' minds, putting the human experience into compelling emotions and provoking thought with a signature humorous storytelling style.

To book Nenshia or send her a message, send an email to:
booking@lexxikhanpresents.com

ABOUT KEAIDY BENNETT

Originally from Honduras, Keaidy Bennett is a best-selling author located in Longwood, Florida.
When Keaidy is not with her children, you can find her reading, writing, or finding ways to help her community. If you want to connect with her, make sure to follow her on Instagram @ akawords

To book Keaidy or send her a message, send an email to:
booking@lexxikhanpresents.com

Made in the USA
Coppell, TX
09 March 2024

29934210R00098